Prince Roman

Also From CD Reiss

Want to know more about Raven's ex - Silicon Valley tycoon Taylor Harden?

Check out *King of Code* !

Raven's world is expanded in two more full-length standalones:

Prince Charming | *White Knight*

More sexy and heartwarming standalones:

Hardball: A pro baseball player falls for a buttoned-up librarian. What could go wrong?

Shuttergirl: An A-list actor is obsessed with a girl from the wrong side of the tracks.

Bombshell: When Hollywood's most available bad boy has a sweet five year-old dropped on his doorstep, he hires the best nanny in town. All he has to do is keep himself from falling in love with her.

Meet your next kinky billionaire obsession in *The Submission Series*.
Submission | *Domination* | *Connection*

What happens when a stuck-up heiress catches the eye of a dangerous mob capo?
Find out in *The Corruption Series*.

Spin | *Ruin* | *Rule*

Celebutante Fiona Drazen lives a life of boundary-free debauchery.
She's utterly forbidden to the one man who can save her.

Kick | Use | *Break*

To keep up with new releases, get on the mailing list!

Prince Roman
By CD Reiss

1001 Dark Nights

EVIL EYE
CONCEPTS

Prince Roman
By CD Reiss

1001 Dark Nights

Copyright 2017 Flip City Media Inc.

ISBN: 978-1-945920-57-8

Foreword: Copyright 2014 M. J. Rose

Published by Evil Eye Concepts, Incorporated

Acknowledgments from the Author

I am so grateful to be a part of the 1,001 Dark Nights family. Laurelin Paige introduced me to Liz Berry and MJ Rose. It was an honor then, and it's an honor now.

Laurelin and Lauren Blakely are my mentors and sisters. I owe them LITERALLY EVERYTHING. Luckily, they'll take repayment in friendship.

I'm a changeling. Liz and her team put up with a lot of crap from me as I changed this story, the title, and the blurb 1,001 times before I got the entire series the way I wanted it. She, Kasi, and Kimberly edited it exactly the way I liked, making it better without changing it into something different.

I am always in my family's debt. I work hard for them and I couldn't do it without them.

And Liz, again. I'm forgetting ten people, but I have to thank Liz three times over for her flexibility as I handed her books, then took them away. You're a good soul and a true patron of this art form.

Sign up for the 1001 Dark Nights Newsletter
and be entered to win a Tiffany Key necklace.

There's a contest every month!

Go to www.1001DarkNights.com to subscribe.

As a bonus, all subscribers will receive a free
1001 Dark Nights story
The First Night
by Lexi Blake & M.J. Rose

One Thousand and One Dark Nights

Once upon a time, in the future...

*I was a student fascinated with stories and learning.
I studied philosophy, poetry, history, the occult, and
the art and science of love and magic. I had a vast
library at my father's home and collected thousands
of volumes of fantastic tales.*

*I learned all about ancient races and bygone
times. About myths and legends and dreams of all
people through the millennium. And the more I read
the stronger my imagination grew until I discovered
that I was able to travel into the stories... to actually
become part of them.*

*I wish I could say that I listened to my teacher
and respected my gift, as I ought to have. If I had, I
would not be telling you this tale now.
But I was foolhardy and confused, showing off
with bravery.*

*One afternoon, curious about the myth of the
Arabian Nights, I traveled back to ancient Persia to
see for myself if it was true that every day Shahryar
(Persian: شهریار, "king") married a new virgin, and then
sent yesterday's wife to be beheaded. It was written
and I had read, that by the time he met Scheherazade,
the vizier's daughter, he'd killed one thousand
women.*

Something went wrong with my efforts. I arrived in the midst of the story and somehow exchanged places with Scheherazade — a phenomena that had never occurred before and that still to this day, I cannot explain.

Now I am trapped in that ancient past. I have taken on Scheherazade's life and the only way I can protect myself and stay alive is to do what she did to protect herself and stay alive.

Every night the King calls for me and listens as I spin tales. And when the evening ends and dawn breaks, I stop at a point that leaves him breathless and yearning for more. And so the King spares my life for one more day, so that he might hear the rest of my dark tale.

As soon as I finish a story... I begin a new one... like the one that you, dear reader, have before you now.

Chapter 1

RAVEN

I never thought about him naked.

Probably because during our affair—which went on for about a year and ended with a whimper seven months earlier—I never saw Taylor fully undressed. We usually met in some dark corner of the office and did little more than expose the relevant body parts.

But the other reason I never thought about him naked was because it just wasn't like that. Brilliant, handsome, ambitious, rich, and about to get much richer, he was a real catch if you could ignore the fact that he was a complete ego-hole. I couldn't ignore it and I couldn't change it. So I'd used him like an in-office vibrator until he came back from a trip with a new girlfriend. I couldn't find a hard feeling about it anywhere.

"Is it money?" he asked, hands folded on his desk. "I promised you a bonus in December. Do you need it now?"

"No."

"If it's not about money...?" He let the sentence hang, hands open as if he wanted me to drop motivations in them. We were always frank with each other, but I didn't have to make his life that easy, did I? He and every other Silicon Valley wunderkind ego-hole had it a little too easy.

"It's not about the other thing either," I said.

"Which other thing?"

He wasn't playing coy. He really did need to know which thing.

"It's not about your new girlfriend or any kind of hard feelings about anything associated with you and me fucking."

"Good, so…"

"And it's not about the fact that you came back from your trip with a ten-point plan for improving the culture in this snake pit, or that it fell on your human resource manager's shoulders."

That was me and those were my shoulders. I really didn't hold a grudge about it, but making him uncomfortable was its own reward.

"Not about you staying late after work six nights a week," I continued, "teaching me how to hack some girl I didn't know, or the four hundred other new responsibilities you laid on me since you got back."

"I laid them on you because I trust you."

"I know. And I appreciate it."

"You're not going to try and hack Neuronet, are you?" Taylor had taught me the basics of hacking, and it had been fun, but I was never going to be as good as him or his partner, Keaton. "Because they have core vulnerabilities," he continued.

"No, Taylor. I'm not going to hack Neuronet."

"Things aren't going to be any easier there. It's a goliath on its way to becoming a behemoth. You're going to get overloaded and ignored. You'll never be ignored here, even after we crush them."

"I'm sure I could be a big shot here in the next ten to twelve years, but here's the thing. We've crunched the numbers. QI4 has challenges."

He leaned back in his chair and crossed his arms. The sleeves of his jacket hiked up, exposing an expensive watch and starched shirt cuffs. He was the only circuit mogul in town who wore suits.

"In five years," he said, "this is going to be the only computer company in the world."

"There's a fifty percent chance you won't be in business in five years."

"Forty-eight percent."

FILE UNDER: SOP mathematical hair-splitting.

Taylor had changed in the past few months, but when he didn't want to hear something, he didn't hear it.

"You're building a vertical rollout that can fall apart at any stage. I don't want to see that happen. I really don't. But I didn't come to Silicon Valley to wake up in five years and have to start over. I need stability."

"Stability and your stock options, I assume?"

"I'd consider it a nice homage to the good times in the supply closet."

His smirk was as wicked as ever.

"Good times."

Chapter 2

RAVEN

As a lover, I hadn't had a future with Taylor, but I'd been attracted to him. Suits, cleanliness, and attention to detail got me off. Ego-holeness didn't.

The only reason I'd ever had a date in Silicon Valley was the pure odds that something had to make sense with someone. After all, I was a highly desired specimen, so rare in the wild that I attracted attention wherever I went. Numbers had been crunched. Articles had been written. The odds of my existence were infinitesimal. In this particular corner of California, I was a unicorn.

Meaning, I was a single female of child-bearing age.

I had my pick.

The guy with the mutton chops he thought were neat-o, or the dude in the Van Halen T-shirt that had the porousness and smell of Swiss cheese. The guy who couldn't stop talking about *World of Warcraft* or the one who mentioned he went to grad school "in Cambridge" four times in four minutes. The experts on beer, custom-tuned guitars, gastropubbing, and social awkwardness. I'd dated boys in men's bodies, humorless geniuses, closet Nazis, and unapologetic sexists who could rattle off the most convenient stats, studies, biological "facts," and "cultural norms" that proved a woman's place was in human resources doing anything but hiring other women.

Taylor had been a pretty good deal, everything considered. He at least showed me enough coding and IT to make me valuable in system implementation.

"But never again," I said to Masy on the walk from the parking lot on the first day. The weather was standard-issue California perfect but seemed just a touch more perfect on the way into my new job. It was going to stay that way. "No more intra-office fucking."

"Trust me," she said, popping her lips off the green straw sticking out of her frothy coffee, "you're safe from dating anyone at Neuronet. It's like a cross-section of the worst of them." My best friend, roommate, and fellow single-female unicorn worked in the marketing department. She'd mentioned the VP opening in HR systems when it opened up. Neuronet was as excited to meet me as I was eager to work with them.

Masy and I shared a two-bedroom apartment in a complex near Market Street. It had two floors, two parking spots, a porch, and a courtyard. We were so busy we were barely ever in the house at the same time. Maybe now we'd find time to hang out.

I'd gotten my ID and had two days of orientation. I'd chosen my health insurance package and enthusiastically signed on to the eight pages of company policy. They had a cutting-edge non-fraternization policy they wrote after an infamous lawsuit. The upshot was simple. The regular folk had a regular fraternization policy that centered around respect and non-harassment. Executives lost their jobs. Period.

I liked that. It would keep my skirt on.

I signed two and a half pages of nondisclosure agreement, and studied a thumb drive describing a complex system called the "information plexus." I'd memorized the flowchart over the weekend. Soft engineering could route the system assurance team anything through nodes A, B, D, and G, and system assurance could tell package design A, B, and G, but not D, whereas if anyone in customer service heard a whisper of A or D, you could rest assured, an ex-employee was getting sued.

I beeped in with my new ID, walked with Masy through the glass-enclosed lobby and into the grassy courtyard with the

Alexander Calder sculpture and the circular amphitheater in poured concrete.

"I'm this way," she said, pointing left with her coffee.

"I'm here." I pointed right. "Thank you again."

"Thank me in five years."

"I will. I know it." I hugged her and went to my new office.

Chapter 3

RAVEN

I barely had a handle on the most direct route to the bathrooms before I was pulled into a meeting by Lonnie, the president of HR. She had been at Neuronet from the beginning, when Alexander Burke started the company out of his parents' kitchen in Menlo Park. She probably had a few hundred million in stock options. She was six inches shorter than me and wider, but she carried herself as if she owned the joint, which—in stock options—she practically did.

"We have outside legal counsel coming in to audit the benchmarking system before implementation," she said, shuffling down the hall, nodding at everyone she passed. "Burke wanted to have some clear-eyed oversight to make sure we hadn't built bias into the system. Every employee, five thousand of us, all will get raises and promotions based on what's input in this system. Since 'Nolan', it's important to get it right or these guys' legal fees are going to be peanuts compared to another settlement."

This system was the reason I'd been hired. Neuronet was still recovering from a pay-bias lawsuit that had cost them nearly a billion dollars.

George Nolan had been fired for releasing a screed about gender roles at Neuronet on his blog. George thought women were mostly (not all) lousy coders and mostly (not all) ill-suited to power positions. He was in the process of suing for wrongful termination and Neuronet was in the process of proving his point had been moot.

It was my job to make sure the implementation was smooth. I had programming experience, thanks to Taylor, and enough HR to know how grading and compensation systems worked. I didn't need a babysitter.

"What's their involvement?"

"Looking over your shoulder and making you crazy."

"We don't have in-house legal?"

"We do, we do. But they went through it already." She stopped before she went around the corner, facing me and speaking gently. "We brought them in to pick it apart from an adversarial vantage. We need it."

"Of course," I replied, deciding not to bristle. It was my first day. "I'll make sure they have all the information they need."

"Good, because they brought in the guy who got the Deton Industries pay-bias settlement."

She led me down the next hall, along a bank of windows to the corner conference room. It was like all the others in stark white, glass, and chrome. One thing was different. The people at the long table.

Not all of the people. They looked like business-casual Silicon Valley lawyers. Suits-no-ties, jacket-and-sneakers, chinos-as-trousers types. One person was different. One man in a perfect gray suit and purple tie. I knew right away he dressed like that every day. He didn't get dolled up for a meeting at Neuronet. This was his five- or six-day-a-week look and it was breathtaking. The way the shoulders looked broad but not padded and the knot of the tie was wide and thick against the spread of his white collar.

He nodded and smiled, tilting his head so the parentheses of light brown hair that escaped into our line of sight didn't come between us.

"This is Roman Bianchi," Lonnie introduced. "He's the team lead."

He held his hand out. Looked me in the eye. Green. Brown. Gray. Was that called hazel? Or had this man invented something completely new? He was proof of unfairness in the world. No one should get to look like that. I'd met good-looking men before, but when he looked at me over our clasped hands and said "Nice to meet you," I forgot what I was supposed to say in response.

Luckily, Lonnie sent my handshake around the table. Five other lawyers. I memorized the names easily and sat down.

"So," Lonnie said, "you've got five here? You'll need space. We'll set you up with terminals—"

"Just me," Roman said. His voice had the flat, passionless intonation of a man relaying not just information, but the fact of every assumption surrounding that information. Just him. No questions necessary. "Jan's staying in our office in Sunnyvale doing data analysis. The rest of the team will be in and out. You should set up a few desks, and if you can spare an office for me, I'd appreciate it."

He smiled at Lonnie and I melted like butter on a skillet. My boss seemed unaffected.

"I can find something for you. You want to be near human resources?"

"Who's my point person?"

"Raven's managing implementation. Give her a few days to get on her feet."

"First day?" he asked me as if asking if I was a virgin. As a matter of fact, when he asked me that, it was the question I heard. *First day?* As if the point of the question was filthy, and he was asking me just how virgin the virgin could be.

"No," I said without thinking. He raised an eyebrow. He knew it was my first day. He'd just been making suggestive small talk. My auto-verbalization script kept running unchecked; "I mean you." *Fuck.* "I mean yes. Yes, it's my first day."

"Well, now that that's straightened out," Lonnie said when everyone was done laughing.

I felt like a fool. That wasn't going to work. Not at all.

Chapter 4

RAVEN

It was late. There was never enough time to meet everyone from every department to note the specific challenges and complaints of every single department leader and member. So I scheduled another seven p.m. meeting. The fourth in the two weeks I'd been at Neuronet. The sky got a little bluer every time as we got deeper into spring, and my attraction to the lawyer on the other side of the table didn't abate one bit.

Lonnie had put Roman in an office right across from mine. There was a narrow hall between us with two desks for assistants. His assistant desk was empty. My assistant was Oona. She came with the job. She knew everything about the company and sat a little to the right so I had a clear view of him.

I wasn't obsessed, necessarily. But I did do a little mild, lightweight hacking I'd learned at QI4. More than I should have done. More than I was comfortable with. But he was pretty tempting, and every time I saw him, I wanted to know more.

FILE UNDER: Friend of Alexander Burke.

FILE UNDER: Mediocre high school record.

I could have asked him, but I remembered the rock solid executive non-fraternization policy and went for the hacks. The policy was strict for executives, but when it came to contractors, it included damages. We were his client, but he was also ours, and there was no tolerance for it.

FILE UNDER: Sky-high LSAT score.

I was up late too many nights digging into Roman Bianchi's life, especially if we'd had a meeting that day. I promised myself I wouldn't do it any more. This would be the last seven p.m. meeting that sent me into the dark web.

Oona asked to be excused to pick up her nephew. Lonnie begged off for her anniversary. The IT point person was optional on the calendar. I grabbed my laptop and bag. I could leave right from the meeting without stopping back at my office. Roman's office was already empty. He was probably waiting in the conference room with his klatch of lawyers.

I rounded the corner and the conference room came into view, but the constellation of lawyers I expected didn't greet me. Just Roman Bianchi, tapping his phone at the head of the table. Enough light came from the windows to keep the fluorescents off, but not enough to keep the twilight from softening the atmosphere around him. I hadn't prepared myself to be alone in a room with him. Hadn't thought I needed to. But when I saw his solitary form, relaxed because he thought no one was looking, I smiled so wide I had to remind myself that uncontrolled giggling was unprofessional.

"Hello." I put my laptop at the opposite end of the table. He looked up from his device.

"Hey." He pivoted, putting his phone down. "You're awfully far away."

"I always sit here."

He indicated the empty seats. "The table's usually lined with people."

I sat and opened my laptop. "Your team's out, too?"

"Apparently."

"Short agenda tonight," I said. "I think we can plow through." If I could just pay attention to the agenda in the first place. I had to start at the top. Breathe. "Item one."

"Skip," he said. "Jan's still working on it."

I checked it off.

"Item two. Product design targets."

He held up his hand. "Problem."

I glanced at him, then clicked my laptop to the relevant section. He was looking at me. Ten tons of hot lawyer funneled into a gaze and weighed on the part of my brain that made words. The clause looked like alphabet soup.

Take your time.

I began, "Design team goals are calibrated against concurrent quarter sales goals in associated departments."

"You can't make the design team responsible for sales goals. We need to minimize variability tied to performance."

I looked over the edge of my screen. He leaned forward on his elbows, laptop closed.

"Why not?"

He folded his hands together in front of him, looking at me across the table, pushing forward. He took my breath away.

"Because product design is sixty percent female. Sales is run by men. You're tying a woman's pay to the performance of men."

I closed my laptop. "That's crazy."

"Sometimes fairness looks crazy."

"You're taking this too far."

He tapped his fingertips together.

"I arbitrated a case at Apex Intel. Small company, but instructive. They'd met gender equity goals by filling their customer service department with women. Coders and engineers were all men. A contingent of their customer service employees sued when their performance surveys started getting downgraded by people calling about faulty programming. You want to know what that cost Apex?"

I slid my laptop away so I could lean forward.

"Three million, of which you took one point two in fees. And your written argument about the way the surveys were structured was brilliant."

"Thank you."

I stood as if I was done with this meeting. "Even if completely immoral."

"I'm not paid by the diocese or the government. You, on the other hand…"

"…are on the way out." I picked up my computer. "I'll see you in the morning."

"Went to USC. Finance. Top honors but ended up in HR."

"I like people. Can't say the same for you, being a video game nerd."

"You beta tested *Harbinger Four*. You should know."

"I was sixteen."

He leaned back and clicked his pen.

"I know."

This motherfucker had hacked me the same way I'd hacked him. Maybe he used the same methods I'd learned from Taylor or maybe he just did lawyer magic. Maybe it was all in the public record, but I was so irritated I could barely see straight. He'd outdone me, and I wouldn't be outdone.

"Why did you miss your graduation from Loyola?" I asked.

"Family obligations."

"I'm sorry about your father."

"That was a long time ago." I was on my way to the door when he continued. "Speaking of fathers, I saw one of your father's sculptures in the lobby at Apple."

I was at his side of the table when he stopped me cold.

"Really?" I put my things down, fully committed to this dick-swinging contest. "There to see your old buddies from the Borden case?"

"Actually, I went to see the sculpture."

"Why?"

"Your father made it. I thought it might give me a little insight into you."

I put my knuckles on the table. He didn't move. Didn't try to empower himself by standing. He just leaned back, letting himself slide down the seat a little. The posture didn't make him smaller. Didn't make him cowed or weak. It made him look more competent and confident. How did he do that?

"Don't you think that's a little weird?"

He tapped the end of his pen against his lips. Was he trying to draw attention to them? Because that was exactly what he was doing.

"I like to know who I'm dealing with."

"Who do you think you're dealing with?"

His head tilted ever so slightly, and his lips curved just a little. The expression was bathed in a subtle sexuality that made me uncomfortable in the most sexy way.

"Someone who left a very lucrative post at a growing disruptor. Our job as outside counsel is to question everything house counsel does. Alexander Burke loved you, and he runs this show. But for us, it's a red flag."

I stepped back so he could stand. I didn't want to be too close to him. I wouldn't be responsible for my actions, except that I would be.

"Really? How's that?"

He slid his computer into his satchel.

"We needed to make sure you left for the reasons you said."

"I did."

"We know."

I had nothing else to say. I picked up my things and opened the door.

He spoke before I was all the way out.

"We should play *Harbinger* some time. I hear *Seven* is trip-A."

"In your arrogant opinion." I used a common gamer phrase. He smiled.

"Indeed." He closed his bag. Even the way he ran the zipper across the top was sexy. "Truthfully, I haven't been that plugged-in since I was a kid."

"Me either."

"But we could have fun."

Fun? With him? The thought sent a rigid tingle up my spine and a liquid throb downward. Was he asking me out? Was he coming on to me? Did he just want to play *Harbinger Seven*? I hadn't even played since the fifth iteration.

It didn't matter what he wanted. It mattered what I wanted.

"I'll see you tomorrow," I said, walking out before he could say another word. I didn't know how much strength I had against him.

Chapter 5

ROMAN

If Raven Crosby hadn't picked up some hacking tips from QI4, I'd eat my shoe.

She'd left as they were growing. Kept her stock options. That never happens. She was also still friendly with Taylor Harden, the hacker brain behind QI4's quantum system.

I figured they'd parted on good terms. Maybe with something hanging over Taylor's head.

My team ended up with a few folders on her. I told myself I was a lawyer. Collecting data on people was what I did for a living.

But this was different.

A week in, I was obsessed with her ebony hair and eyes. Lashes drawn on with black Sharpie. Her voice was hypnotic in meetings, and was only heard after long stretches of listening. The night before, she'd tipped her hand, showing me that she'd peeled the curtain back to get intel on me. I didn't feel violated as much as vindicated. The attraction was mutual. She wouldn't have done it for any other reason.

"I'll be there at eight," I said to my sister, Teagan. We had a dinner planned half an hour before, but I didn't want to go. It wasn't the rain that pounded on the windows. It wasn't my sister. Teagan was fine, but the office was empty and Raven was right across the hall, working in the glow of a desk lamp.

"You better be," she said. "I'm starving and I need to get drunk."

"Get a head start at the bar."

"I'm not going to sit at the end of the bar by myself with a drink. Do you even know what it's like out there for a girl?"

I didn't know firsthand, obviously, but I knew enough from her. Teagan was a career gamer and game designer. One of the best. She had a sweet, harmless face that made her approachable to even the most beta of betas. Regardless, even the betas tried to compete with her once they knew what she did. I was exhausted on her behalf.

Across the hall, Raven stood and clicked off her desk lamp.

"Leaving now," I said, cutting the call. I grabbed my things and headed out, timing it perfectly so we met in the hall.

"Hi," I said.

She nodded and gave me a non-committal smile. We spoke often, but never a word that didn't have to do with the human resources software implementation and how it would protect Neuronet from liability.

"It's raining," I said. "You taking the elevator to the parking lot?"

The executive lot was underground, on the other side of campus. If you wanted to get there underground, without crossing the courtyard and getting rained on, you had to take the elevator.

"Yes." She started down the hall and I followed.

"I'll walk you."

She looked me up and down, Sharpie lashes fluttering. "Do you have an umbrella? You'll need it."

"Ah." I patted my pockets like a dumbass who lost his keys, not an umbrella.

"I have an extra right inside my office door."

"No, I have one." I stepped backward down the hall. "I'll just go get it."

"Great. See you tomorrow!"

She hurried down the hall as if she'd just dodged three painful minutes in my company.

I shook it off. What was the difference? What was I trying to do here? Get my ass fired? Get her fired? There were dozens of women I could take to bed and absolutely no reason to focus on the one who could make my life and my job miserable.

But that body. The way she walked. The swing of her black hair across her back.

A female voice came from behind me. "There are rumors about that one."

It was Marie Siska. Founding partner at Siska + Welton. She was in her early fifties and had her brown hair up in a tidy twist. She was a former litigator who had argued in front of the Ninth and had a way of knowing the intricacies of every case we handled.

"What kind of rumors?"

"The unsubstantiated kind."

She invited me into my own office and closed the door behind us. I sat in front of my own desk, in one of the two guest chairs.

Marie's lavender pants suit was custom made and she never sat down. She put her hands on the back of the second guest chair, pulling herself up a little as if she wanted to look taller.

"Barney and I have made a decision about you."

I tried to look completely calm, but there was a pretty good chance my face froze over in the attempt.

"Let's hear it."

"Alexander Burke and Neuronet are your catch. If you go, he goes with you. That's a plus in the senior partner column."

I'd played MMPORGs with Burke way back in the day. All the zombie shooting had paid off. He was also a great guy and a badass gamer.

"But we're a recent contract," she continued. "And it's short term. He can cut us loose any time for another outside contractor or to keep it all in-house. It's fine. It's part of the business, but a long-term retainer could be big for us. One third of future billing."

"And my name would be one third of the ones on the letterhead."

She did something she never did. She sat down in front of me. "I've wanted to be a lawyer ever since I saw a Senate debate on C-SPAN. We're a small, classy operation with a stellar reputation. Classy and stellar were the goal, but small wasn't. We should be litigating in front of the Supreme Court, and the reason we're not is because we have to scratch and claw every quarter. We can't take the chances we need to. I have ten or fifteen more years of active participation in this business before I can't keep up, and it's coming at me fast. We've tried to grow and it's never stuck. This is our chance to turn this firm into what I dreamed about when I was ten. You are our chance."

"No pressure."

"None." She got on her feet, where she was most comfortable. "I need you to find a way to be indispensable. If we want to stay, we have to be of value. If we're going to be of value, we have to do more than the job. Then we'll reprint the stationery."

I stood with her. She was offering me my own heart's desire on a plate. Her partner was sixty-four. She'd retire way before me. It would be my firm to run if I could just find a way to keep Neuronet.

Keeping clients was about relationships. I was friends with Alexander Burke, but I needed good connections on the ground. Piece of cake.

I'd get close to Raven.

Professionally, of course.

Chapter 6

RAVEN

Oona had a thick Afro and deep brown skin she didn't need makeup to smooth. She was wildly efficient, painfully honest, and continually communicative.

"I wish I could turn my desk around," she said, handing me a stack of printouts. Her setup kept her back toward my office. "I can't look at him all day. I feel like I'm cheating on Brice."

Through my windows, across the hall, and through Roman's office windows, I could see over the city of Palo Alto all the way to the other side of the bay. But Oona had a point. That wasn't the best view from where we were. The view at the moment was Roman looking out the window with one hand in his pocket and the other with his phone to his ear. The silhouette over the long view of the city was enough to make me press my knees together. One day the implementation would be done and I wouldn't have to look at him any more or avoid him in the cafeteria. I wouldn't have to look away whenever he made eye contact, or avoid laughing at one of his jokes in a meeting.

"You can turn it," I said.

She tightened her lips and shook her head. "Company's very strict on that."

"Uniformity."

"Yeah. But, hot damn." She glanced across the hall, where

Roman had gotten off the phone, and back to me. "Sorry, that's not very professional."

"I won't write you up." I smiled at her, but we weren't supposed to talk like that about associates, no matter how gorgeous they were. "But if you'd be more comfortable moving your computer, you should."

"Great idea."

I flipped through the printout, but Oona stayed by my desk.

"Anything else?"

"Yeah, actually." She lowered her voice. "Do you ever wonder why they put a white dude in charge of overseeing equal compensation?"

"He did arbitration on the Apex case."

"Ah."

"And he's got a history with Burke."

"Knock, knock." The male voice was accompanied by quick-knuckled raps on my open door. It was Roman, eyes greener in the morning sun. It was really hard to breathe when he looked at me. "Raven, do you have a minute?"

He and I acted as though we hadn't weaponized each other's personal information. I pretended I never heard him ask me to have fun gaming and he acted as if he never said it. Not because I wished he hadn't asked, but because the prospect of seeing him socially was so appealing. He was hard to talk to when my body kept reacting to the clear-as-air smell of his aftershave and the cut of his suit.

I avoided him. I didn't want to lose this job doing with Roman what I'd done with Taylor. I wanted stock options and a pension.

But I had a minute and he and I were working together.

"Sure," I said. Oona left.

He and I always met in conference rooms with teams present. But here he was, in my office, and there went Oona, out the door to her own desk. We were alone.

He sat in the chair across the desk, leaning back with his ankle on his knee. Ribbed socks. Sage green. Tan shoes. Gray suit.

It worked. He worked. He was put together like a masterpiece. Oona leaned into the room and started to close the glass door.

"You can leave it open," I said. She nodded and went left

down the hall to pick up more printouts.

Roman tilted his chin to the stack on my desk. "Funny how you still want paper in a digital company."

"The digital reporting capsule hasn't been uploaded," I said, making it a specific point to not look at the way his hand curved around the edge of the armrest, or the way his watch peeked past his cuff, or the way his shirt stretched across his chest.

He nodded. "I wanted to talk about that."

His eyes were on my face. Completely appropriate, but when he looked at me like that I felt naked.

I didn't want this kind of energy at Neuronet. I'd dealt with enough of it in my first couple of weeks. On any normal day, from any normal man, I'd feel both violated and annoyed. But he was different. He didn't repel me. He did the opposite, no matter how professional he was. I lost myself.

What was I wearing? I couldn't remember.

"Reporting's not in your plexus," I said.

You're wearing the burgundy skirt suit.

"Well, maybe."

And the pink blouse...

"If you want to open up a node, I can get you the information management forms."

...with the third button that pops open when you don't want it to...

"Here's my point," he said, eyes in only the most appropriate places. "You're new. I'm new. I have no idea how you work."

...and the hot pink bra...

"Why is that important?"

...that scratches your nipples when they get hard.

"Process is everything."

Don't think about it.

"The software measures results."

Do. Not. Think. About. It.

"We're two ships passing in the night," he said, and I imagined a pause after, but it might have been just my imagination. "Unless legal fully understands how results are tabulated and understood by management, we can't offer an accurate recommendation."

His gaze flicked lower for a brief second and my chest—which was hopefully under a fully buttoned shirt—tingled with prickly heat and the lace scratched where I was sensitive.

"We can set up a series of meetings," I said, hoping I wouldn't have to.

"If I sit in one more meeting, I'm going to throw my degree in the trash and join the circus."

I laughed, forgetting my blouse for a second. He smiled when I did and for the first time, Roman Bianchi seemed approachable.

"Let's just have a lunch in the cafeteria." He took his ankle off his knee and leaned forward. "See how we start approaching this."

The laughter had caught me off guard.

"Sure. How about Friday?"

He looked at his watch and leaned back, calling out the open door. "Oona?"

She appeared. "Yes?"

"Does Raven have anything on the calendar for lunch today?"

"Nope."

"Great. Thank you." He stood up as if it was all decided. "I have an eleven-thirty. Meet you at one by the Big Circuit."

When he left, I very calmly put my hand to my chest. All my buttons were fastened. I laughed a little at myself. Silly, silly girl.

I had to work with him, and as the months went on, I was going to have to work more and more closely. My hard nipples and flushed skin were going to become problems.

I was giving Roman power over me. Yes, he was fine on the eyes. He dressed well and carried a power and confidence about him that turned me on. He wore his competence like a suit of armor.

The only way to break down my attraction was to make him human. I could do that. I'd done it before.

First step, get to know him and all his most unattractive traits. Knock him down a few pegs and he'd just become another coworker.

Yeah. I could do that.

Chapter 7

ROMAN

The Big Circuit was off the back of the cafeteria. It was a vertical topiary climbing a thin steel plate. The branches and flowers and whatnot made it look like a circuit. Water flowed to make more lines and connections. It had a few green metal tables around it and since the sky was cloudy and the air was cool, I figured it wouldn't be too crowded.

I got there first. That was intentional. It would be easier for her if she was the one approaching and standing. I'd let her dictate the pace and volume of the opening. This was important. She needed to feel safe, because in her office a few hours before, a couple of things had become clear.

One, I made her uncomfortable.

Two, she was attracted to me.

Was one the result of two? Or the other way around? Or were they separate?

I had to know. In the most unprofessional way...I had to know.

I stood when she came out with her tray.

"Hi," she said. "Did you get the chicken?"

I pulled the chair out for her. She swallowed. I wasn't supposed to do that. We were professionals and equals, but I had habits instilled in me I wasn't breaking. Fuck that.

"We're not on a date, Mr. Bianchi."

"You're holding the tray with two hands, Ms. Obvious."

She laughed. When I'd made the circus crack that morning her laugh almost broke through every last shred of professionalism I'd had. It wasn't some unique snort or a sun-just-came-through-the-clouds kind of thing. It was perfectly normal. The gratification came from the fact that I'd created it.

She sat.

"What did you get?" I asked. The cafeteria was run by a full-time professional chef and staffed so fully that they could put out one perfectly plated serving at a time.

"The tikka masala."

"I got the generic chicken."

"Do you not like the food here?" she asked. I noticed she'd only brought a small notebook, and her phone was in her pocket. If she'd prepared for this meeting, I couldn't see it.

"Better than the firm's. We have a vending machine with ramen noodles and granola bars."

"That sounds terrible."

"It's fine. My mother was a complete hack." I cut my chicken. "I mean, I love her and all. She's my mother. But she boiled pasta to a paste. When it got cold, my sister and I cut it into slices."

"Come on. Really?"

I was amusing her. Total dopamine rush.

"We had sliced spaghetti sandwiches for lunch."

"Stop."

Laughing a little now.

"With ketchup." I popped a piece of very non-generic chicken into my mouth. "Does a body good."

Her smile was genuine, and that too was a natural high.

"And did you miss it when you left Oakland?" Her question was a shameless admission that she knew where I was from. Fair enough. We'd already gone down the path of admitting we'd researched each other.

"Not a bit. You miss Austin's weirdness?"

"It's only weird for Texas."

"You don't have an accent."

"Funny. You do."

Touché, lovely woman. Touché. I was forgetting myself, my surroundings, my purpose in being there.

"What brung ya?" I spun my fork at the Palo Alto sky, Silicon Valley, the entire Bay area.

She put her eyes on her plate, stabbing her food so hard the plastic plate clacked.

"Someone already killed that chicken," I said.

She smiled. Man, I liked that smile.

"I came with a guy named Aiden. He developed HearThis, which I'm sure you've heard of."

"That got sold to Niles Havershim, right?"

"Yeah. Then he dumped me. Which is more than you need to know."

"And why did you stay in paradise?"

She shrugged. "My parents are artists. We lived in a van until I was eight. We were always hand to mouth or like, if my dad sold a sculpture it was great for a bit, but if my mother didn't have a tour one year, which was pretty common, it was ramen and granola bars."

"They must have stocked the vending machines in my office."

"That would require business sense, which they don't have and never will. I'm not judging because I didn't get any either. Not for my own business. I'm happy in a regular gig and my best option was to stay here. Get a stable job. Be a grown-up."

"You grew up nice." I think I said it with a little too much conviction. She put her hand to the top button of her blouse. Maybe not too much conviction. Maybe too much subtext.

"You shouldn't say stuff like that," she said. "It could create the wrong impression."

"This is the first time you've told me anything personal. Something tells me if I were a woman, I'd know something about you."

"So?"

"Don't you think that might create the wrong impression?"

Her glance was just a tick to the left of flirty, and the way she tilted her head to expose her neck was just to the right side of sensual. My dick reacted. Biology is powerful. But it wasn't just my dick. My brain decided it was time to shatter a solid brick wall wrapped in corrugated steel behind a hard-earned filter that separated the appropriate from the inappropriate.

My plan to make her laugh was breaking down and I had no control over it. None. I was my own worst enemy. Everything I'd been bottling up came out all at once.

"Your neck's broken out in spots." I leaned forward so I could speak softly. "You're fondling your fork like it's a kitten."

Shut up, asshole.

"Your legs are crossed, but I bet in another place—"

No, really, shut up.

"—another time—"

There's no going back from this.

"—I could get you to open them."

Her fork clattered to the plate. Grains of rice bounced onto the tabletop. She stood like a shot.

"This meeting is over."

As much as I usually enjoyed watching her walk away, I kept my eyes on my plate.

If she thought she was shocked at my behavior, I was ten times as surprised.

What was wrong with me?

Chapter 8

RAVEN

I didn't see Roman for the rest of the day, which was a goddamn good thing. Getting to know him so I could be less attracted to him was backfiring spectacularly.

And yes, I was deeply offended at the lines he'd crossed over lunch.

But I was also turned on. All through afternoon evaluations, I was deeply, uncomfortably engorged and wet. I was glad I'd worn a skirt because the crotch of my panties was wet enough to soak through.

As the VP of human resources, I taught classes on company policy, diversity, and sexual harassment, and I'd been sexually harassed at lunch.

But it didn't feel like sexual harassment. It felt like foreplay.

And since feeling harassed was part of the definition, and because I never told him not to tell me he could open my legs at some point in the future, I chalked it up to a fair game attempt that couldn't be repeated.

"You are the face of the department," I said to myself as I tapped out an email. "They'll fire you if you don't get a hold of this shit."

Mr. Bianchi:

Thank you for joining me for lunch.

As a matter for the record, you have pursued me up to the limit I find appropriate.

Please cease immediately. Any verbal or physical advances will be considered harassment from this point forward.

Though this email is an official correspondence, it will not be shared unless it becomes necessary by your continued pursuit.

Best Regards,

Raven Crosby
VP of Human Resources
The Neuronet Corporation

I thought hard before sending it.

FILE UNDER: You might live to regret this.

He was funny and handsome. He was powerful and confident. When I thought of lying back as he spread my knees apart, a shot of pleasure ran along the seam between my legs.

But I'd have to quit. No one quit Neuronet. They made sure you stayed, and I wanted to stay. I wanted one last steady job between now and retirement. Roman Bianchi wasn't the last man on earth.

I sent it, and my email pinged immediately afterward. I froze.

If he said "fine, no problem" would that be okay? Would I be disappointed?

To hell with it. I needed to cut this thing off while I was strong.

It was Masy.

Ravey Baby—
Boom.
Jude gave me tickets for SSV—video game soundtracks.
8 pm
See you there.
M

Jude was the head of the Neuronet marketing department.

SSV was the Symphony Silicon Valley.

Video game soundtracks rearranged for a full orchestra was a first for the symphony, and tickets were impossible to get, which was why Masy assumed I could make it.

"Oona!" My assistant darted in.

"Yes!"

"Do I have anything tonight after 6:30?"

"No."

"Good, I'm leaving. I got seats at the SSV!"

"Tonight? Brice is taking me!"

"Maybe I'll see you there." I closed my laptop. The symphony and a few friendly faces would be the perfect distraction.

Chapter 9

RAVEN

"Would you say this is baroque or rococo?" I asked Masy. The lobby was dipped in gold and draped in red velvet.

"I have no idea what you're talking about." She swirled her whiskey sour, trying to free the cherry from under the ice. She and I wore the best things we had in our closets. I was in a fitted floor-length with bronze sequins in a paisley pattern. She wore a purple cocktail dress that showed off her long legs.

Naturally, we were overdressed compared to the rest of the crowd.

"Stylistic eras. The price of having artist parents. Never mind." I poked my vodka rocks with the skinny red straw, pushing the lemon out of the way. I drained the glass down to the last unmelted drop.

"You did the right thing," she said, leaning in so she could be heard over the recordings of the SSV doing *Harry Potter* and *Lord of the Rings*. I'd told her about Roman in the car. I'd told her about what he'd said and my email response.

"I know."

Masy had a boyfriend. He worked at Google and she never saw him. She never complained about it and seemed perfectly happy when they were together.

"You look like you're having second thoughts," she said.

"When I told you the story...I skipped a part."

Her eyes went a little wide as she filled in the blanks with my history and her own assumptions.

"You didn't."

"No. But I have to be honest. He's really... I got a little turned on."

"Okay, look." She put her empty glass on a cocktail table as if she needed both hands free to make her point. "You're attracted to men in power. Okay? This is your thing. So you have to just meet a man in power at a different company, and you're only going to be able to do that if you get out of the office once in a while. Am I right?"

"I know. That's why I switched jobs."

"Right."

"QI4 was just this self-perpetuating nightmare even before Taylor came back."

"Right. So you took a first step. And now the universe is testing you. It's asking you how much you're really committed to having and keeping a stable job. And you're committed, right?"

"I am."

"And you're not going to have sex with a guy in the office, right?"

"Right. No matter how much I want to."

"Eyes on the prize."

"Eyes on the prize." I nodded, putting my empty glass next to hers like a punctuation mark. Masy hooked her arm in mine and led me to the center of the room.

"Let's find you a nice man. How about that one? He's hot."

Mr. Hot checked us out as we passed and smiled a perfect, handsome smile.

"He's wearing a hoodie to the symphony."

Masy sighed and shook her head. "So picky. Silver Fox at one o'clock?"

Mr. Fox was well put together. He stood straight and would have been a possibility until he raised his glass to his lips.

"Wedding ring," I said.

"You need a nice VC guy. Let's see if I can sniff one out." She craned her neck. I was thinking about getting another drink in before the show started when a shot of liquid cold ran down my back. I squealed in shock, spinning around.

A woman my age in a layered magenta skirt and turquoise tank made a squinched-up face, holding up her hands. One had a drink in it.

"I'm so sorry!" A lock of curly blue hair fell over one eye. "Someone pushed me."

I twisted to see the damage, but couldn't get around that far.

"It was a Witch's Tit," Blue Hair said. "Vodka and other clear stuff."

Masy stepped behind me. "Looks all right. Just wet."

"I'm sorry!" Blue Hair said again. "I'll give you my number and I'll pay for dry cleaning."

"It's all right," I said, feeling the warming liquid soak downward. She must have dumped half a glass on me.

The background music faded out and a bell rang. Five minutes to take our seats. I didn't have time to go to the bathroom to dab this dry.

"You're such a klutz," a man's voice said. I spun around to see where it came from, because I recognized it.

"Roman." His name was a flat statement. He had his hand on Blue Hair's shoulder and a totally appropriate goddamn suit. He was distractingly gorgeous in the office. Outside it, he was the only man in the room.

And he was with a woman already. I didn't know if I was angry or jealous.

"Raven." His voice was as flat as mine.

I was jealous. I had no business being jealous. Primarily, I should have been enraged on her behalf, because he was with her and he'd hit on me six hours earlier. But I was as jealous as a jilted high schooler with a prom date caught kissing someone else by the lockers. I was losing my mind.

"Well," Masy interjected. "This is fun. But we have to take our seats." She grabbed me but I yanked away. I wanted to get control of this moment and the blood-boiling possessiveness I had no business feeling.

"I have to go clean up." I turned to Blue Hair and her date, who I tried hard to not look at. I really tried. I practically had to count the blue hairs. "It's fine. Please don't worry about it. I had to dry clean it anyway." I addressed Roman, though I kept my eyes on his tie, because if I looked him in the eye I'd fall down the abyss of gray green and drown. "Enjoy the show."

The crowd headed to either side of the lobby and the stairs; I went against traffic to the First Street side of the building. The restroom was clearing out, but someone behind me was in a hurry to get in. As I was about to push the door open, a hand went around my waist, and I knew who it was.

I elbowed Roman, which did exactly nothing.

"What do you want?" I growled.

He led me away from the bathroom. The hall was almost completely clear of people. "Come with me."

"Why should I?"

He cut a turn into a narrower hall and spun with his finger out as if he wanted to accuse me of something terrible.

"Because I want to apologize."

I crossed my arms, savoring his humiliation. "For?"

"For telling you how I really felt at the wrong place and time."

"So you're apologizing for the circumstances?"

"I'm not going to apologize for wanting you."

A glowing warmth spread across my body. In the symphony hall, away from the office, dressed in clothes meant to promise sex without guaranteeing it, his desire was flattering. Even welcome.

"You're a creep."

"My apology is honest."

"Screw your honesty. You have no business being honest about wanting me when you're with someone."

He looked surprised for a split second, as if he forgot who he walked through the door with.

"You're a pig," I continued.

Eyebrows raised, somehow more confident than he had any business being.

"Let me straighten you out, Raven Crosby. That woman I came with is Teagan White. She goes by—"

"White_Girl22? You came with White_Girl22 and you want what out of me?"

Bianchi is White in Italian.

I knew what he was going to say before he said it.

"She's my sister."

There it was.

He was single and we weren't at work. He'd apologized for the stupid, stupid thing he'd said at lunch, and here we were. Alone. He was gorgeous and vulnerable and here with his sister.

I took one step toward him and he took the sign as if it was in neon paint. Which it was. Neon paint with klieg lights. It said kiss me.

Before I could complete the thought, I was against the wall and his lips were on mine. There was a fierceness to his mouth, a hunger that was the opposite of cold professionalism. His tongue fed me and his hands owned me. I could have melted into him so easily. I could have given myself over and loved every minute of it. I wanted to. My body wanted to. Every nerve in my body vibrated for him.

I pushed him hard and we separated, gasping.

He spoke first, drawing his thumb against the corner of his mouth. "Now, about that email?"

"What about it, Mr. Bianchi?"

Through the walls and far away, the concert started with a classical rendition of Pac-Man music.

"It was clearly false."

The fact that he was right notwithstanding, he was full of it.

"You are now doing what every single stalker, creep, sexual harasser ever does. You have exactly no business near an HR department or a law degree or a woman, for that matter. These tactics don't work. You are not entitled to me or my time."

He didn't answer right away. His expression changed a hundred times in five seconds. Frustration. Anger. Bargaining. Denial. Depression. Acceptance.

"You're right."

"Damn right." I knew I seemed really resolute, because my words reflected the Raven of six seconds before, not the Raven who was processing something completely new and unexpected.

Regret.

I wanted to say yes.

"Roman," I called when he was halfway down the empty hall. He stopped and half-turned. Even with the ornate décor, the deep red carpet, and the polished gold filigree, he was the most captivating thing in my sight.

"Report me or don't," he called back.

"I have another idea." I strode to him, the back of my dress now simply damp instead of damp and cold.

He put his hands in his pockets.

"I know why you did this." I crossed my arms.

"To apologize. I needed to after what I said."

"Yes. You're an asshole."

"I'll take my lumps, Raven. I won't take abuse."

I took a deep breath and answered him in an exhale.

"One night."

"One night?" He took his hands out of his pockets and crossed his arms.

"You and me. Just get it out of our system. And then we drop it and go back to work."

He raised an eyebrow. "It's that easy?"

"I've..." Another deep breath. "I was involved a man I worked with. It's turned out fine. I can compartmentalize."

"What if I can't?"

"Then this isn't a good offer for you."

"I have a condition," he said.

"Okay."

He held up a finger. "One night."

"Yes."

"Until morning."

"What about work?" I asked. "The job?"

"It's Friday," he said. "We start now."

Now? Either he wanted to get it over with so he could start compartmentalizing or he was trying to get me in bed before I changed my mind.

"After the concert," I said. "We can—"

"Now," he interrupted.

Why not? Maybe I was the one who needed to get it over with. I didn't have to drag it out the way I had with Taylor or Aiden. I was more than capable of emotional detachment, and it wasn't like he could hold anything over me at work. I was, in effect, his equal in the office. A warm sense of finality softened the tension in my chest. It was decided, then.

"Now." I unfolded my arms.

He unfolded his arms and we took a step toward each other.

"Are you sure?" he asked when he was a breath's distance.

"Are *you*?"

"I'm sure."

"Tick-tock, then."

His approach was different than it had been before. He took a second to scan my face, to place the tips of his thumbs on my arms and run them over my skin.

"I've wanted you from the minute I saw you."

I put my hands flat on his chest, getting used to the idea of him as a physical, solid presence. I was going to enjoy this one night.

"You made a crack about it being my first time."

"I wanted to bend you over the table." He kissed me with a pop. "Yank your skirt up." Another kiss. "And stick my fingers in you to see if you were wet."

"I was."

"Good."

He gave me his tongue, guided me with his lips, possessed me with his mouth.

FILE UNDER: Kissing.

SUBFOLDER: New benchmark.

Chapter 10

ROMAN

Her roommate had driven, so it was my car and my place. She was on some birth control implant thing, so we didn't have to stop to pick up condoms. Thank God. I couldn't have waited.

In the passenger seat of my Jaguar, she finished texting her roommate and tucked her phone in her jacket pocket.

"Did you tell her who you were with?" I asked.

"She'll be discreet."

She smiled at me and waggled her eyebrows.

We were fifteen minutes from my place. All I wanted to do was pull over and fuck her in my car. I put my hand on her knee and slid her skirt up. No progress. It was down to the floor.

"Want to do something fun?"

"I thought that was what we were doing?"

At a red light, I pinched the sequined fabric. "Pull this up around your waist."

Her eyes glinted in the streetlamps. She bit her lower lip, hesitating.

"Did you think you were in for one time in missionary position and eight hours of sleep?"

"I hope not."

"Good."

"Because I sleep ten hours at a clip."

The light turned green. I went through. Next to me, I sensed her shuffling, heard the rustle of fabric and the creak of strain on her seatbelt. When I glanced to the side, her skirt was just above the top lace of her stockings. I put my hand on her thigh. Felt the silk stockings. The lace. The skin. The garter strap. I slid my finger under it.

"I like this."

"I'm glad."

"Spread your legs."

I got on the freeway. She parted her knees, making room for my hand. The skin inside her thighs was warm and soft. I slipped my pinkie under her panties. She gasped. I hadn't even gotten between the lips yet, but the top of my finger felt the dampness of the fabric. An almost painful pressure built beneath my balls. I was driving. I didn't want to die on the way to my place.

"You're turned on," I said.

"Yes." She took my wrist and pushed my hand between her lips so I could feel how wet she was. Bold. She was so damn bold. I sucked air through my teeth and explored her. "Feel how much I want to fuck."

If the freeway had been a little more crowded, I would have crashed the car.

I pulled my hand away and exited the freeway.

"You—" I pointed to her without looking at her. "You're going to get the fucking of your life tonight. I'm going to fuck your mouth. Your pussy from the front, then the back. I'm going to eat you alive then fuck you again."

"You missed a spot." She reached for the strained fabric over my erection. I stopped her.

"You're filthy. Has anyone ever told you that?"

"Yes."

"Touch yourself, but don't come. Do it with your heels on the seat."

She slid out of her shoes and put her heels on the seat, knees bent. I couldn't see between her legs, but she was exposed. Knowing that was enough to thread more blood though my cock.

Stopping at a light a few blocks from my house, I looked over at her. Bent knees. Hand between her legs. Eyes dark and cheeks highlighted red from the stoplight. The neighborhood was quiet and the street was dead, but we were close to the crosswalk and someone could pull up next to us. Normally, I'd find that hot, but she didn't want us to be that public.

Also, tonight was mine alone.

I gently pushed her knee down, and she dropped the other.

"Hold that thought."

"Holding," she replied. The light went green.

I pulled into my driveway six minutes later.

Chapter 11

RAVEN

I didn't think I'd ever been so wet in my life. And once I started touching between my legs, I got more than simply aroused. I needed it. Needed his dick. Needed to feel him everywhere. Inhibition went out the window.

He pulled past the gate set into high hedges. The gate clanged behind me and he put the car in park in front of the small suburban house.

He got out without a word. I shifted my skirt down so I didn't step out of the car looking like a wrung-out towel. I had one shoe on when my door opened. Looking up, Roman's crotch was about eye level, his face above, burning with intensity. He held out his hand.

Fuck.

The outline of his cock.

I was taking this night for all it was worth.

Jamming my foot into the second shoe, I took his hand and stood. He slammed the door shut, then slammed me against it, kissing me as if he wanted to break me, and without question, I wanted to be broken like a twig.

He shifted my shawl away until there was only dress fabric between my nipples and the spring air. They hardened even more, and when he pinched them through the sequined silk, I grunted like a wild thing.

I grabbed for his belt.

He tugged at my dress.

I felt the warm, taut skin of his cock.

He got my underwear halfway down my thighs.

He pushed me against the cold steel of the car.

I wrapped my legs around him, and he grabbed my panties and ripped the lace apart.

He slid his shaft along the length of my seam.

I was crazed. Wild. Clutching his chest through his shirt.

When he entered me, we both froze for a second.

It had happened so fast, from driving on the freeway to fucking against his car.

I didn't feel my fingers getting cold as much as I stopped feeling my grip on him. As if reading my mind, he hoisted me up and kissed me as he carried me to the house, holding me against the wall with one hand and unlocking the side door with the other. We banged on walls, knocked over a broom, kicked a planter. We wound up lying between the tiles of the dark kitchen and the outside steps.

I leveraged my feet against opposite sides of the doorframe. He went deep, pushing his whole body against me. I cried out his name.

"Say it again."

"Roman. More, more…" I devolved into sounds that didn't make words as he took me slow and hard. Not one stroke was taken for granted. I was a balloon ready to burst, stretching, pumped full.

"You're close," he said.

"Yes."

"Wait for me."

"Don't stop."

I waited. I thought about the Neuronet matrix and employee benchmarks. But the matrix pulsed and the benchmarks counted to his rhythms.

"I'm going to come inside you."

"Now?"

"Yes."

"Ah, y—" I never finished the word. When I felt the pulse at the base of his cock and his face relaxed, I let go. Every muscle in my body tightened toward where we were joined, clamping like a drawstring and releasing into blissful, mindless pleasure.

* * * *

He'd laid me on the bed like a precious item and went for water. I peeled off my bunched-up dress. The view outside was too dark to see through the wood blinds, but I caught the sounds of crickets and rustling tree branches.

Taking a quick inventory of the room, flat screen, three gaming consoles, nonfiction books on the nightstand—*Extra Lives* and *Why Games Matter*. Another called *Advanced Mountaineering*. They matched the photos of nature, mountains, Teagan and him ornamented with carabiners and straps.

FILE UNDER: Well-rounded.

When he came in with two glasses of water he just said…

"Wow."

I got so engaged in his life that I forgot I was wearing nothing but a bra and garter.

"Oh, this old thing?"

He put the glasses down and unbuttoned his cuffs, staring up and down my body in a way he didn't at work. Good thing, too, because wherever his eyes went, my skin tingled as if he was touching it.

"You always wear a garter?"

"Usually."

"Even at work?"

"It makes me feel sexy."

He pulled his shirt over his head, leaving me with a view of his body that was less gamer and more mountaineer than I could have hoped for. I reached for him, laying my hand on his chest.

"From now on," he said. "I'm going to see you in the office and want to rip your sensible little suit off."

"That would be against policy." I drew my nails down his chest and over his hard abs.

"My cock can't read the handbook."

"I'm going to have to have a conversation with your cock, then." I ran my hand over his erection.

"How's that getup look when you're on your knees?" he said softly into my cheek.

"You'll have to let me know."

I got on my knees, looking up at him. His hair slid down when he looked back at me. I took him in my hands and couldn't help smiling.

"I am so good at this," I said.

"Your confidence will reflect positively in your evaluation."

It was hard to get my tongue on him with that grin on my face, but I managed. I didn't want to overpromise and under deliver. I ran my tongue along his shaft, tasting myself, then lowered my mouth onto him. I sucked, drew it out, looked up to check on him. I sucked again, opening my throat and taking a little more. I went at my own pace, until he took the hair on the back of my head and set the rhythm.

"You are—" he gasped. "So good at this."

"More," I said and took him again. He grunted, sucked in air, and pulled away. Grabbing me gently under the arms, he directed me to the bed. I sat on the edge and wiped my chin, watching him step out of his pants. He was so perfect. So stunning. So perfectly commanding as he knelt in front of me and pulled my legs apart and kissed inside my thighs.

"Roman," I said.

"Yes, Raven."

"I'm going to come if you do that."

"We're trading fair and square. Lie back."

I did, and he ran his tongue inside my thighs, spreading me apart, kissing and sucking everything surrounding my seam. His finger slid where his tongue hadn't gone. I was so wet, and just a little sore from the first fuck of the night.

He kissed my clit and I squeaked with pleasure.

"That's nice," he said, pushing two fingers inside me. I was sure it was nice for him, but my entire world was revolving around the movements of his fingers inside me. "I'm going to suck your clit now. You ready?"

The words alone were enough to send me into twitches of anticipation. As if he knew it, he went slowly, watching me with gray-green eyes. His tongue flicked on me once, twice, then he ran his lips over it.

"Oh, God, Roman. It's too much. I'm going crazy."

Unpressured, he kissed and flicked with the promise of more, without the delivery. I was nearly in tears, begging in half sentences, until he pressed his lips around my clit and, ever so gently, sucked on it.

It was the longest orgasm I'd ever had. When it was finished, it wasn't finished. He flipped me over, hitched up my butt, and fucked me from behind.

Then it was all over. I was drained of every last bit of my orgasm, and he came inside me, dropping over me when he was done as if he was completely spent.

"You're going to make this really hard to limit to one night," I said.

"I haven't even started."

Chapter 12

ROMAN

If you can't sleep, eat. If you can't eat, sleep.
Good advice from my dad, who had learned it in the Army. Since my night with Raven had gone deep into the early morning hours, and since I always woke up hungry anyway, I figured I'd make a big breakfast.

The first thing about a meal like that is you have to time everything right. You can't start the eggs first or they'll get to the table cold, but you can't scramble them right before you're going to put them in the pan or you're going to get behind on the pancakes. Condiments go out first so the syrup flows and the butter is soft enough to spread on toast that's going to be hottest while you might be pulling the bacon out of the oven.

It ran like a military operation if done right, and for the same reason climbing gear needed to be packed in a certain order. Time didn't wait for anyone.

Choreographing all the moving parts took up 75 percent of my attention, and when she came down showered and dressed in her sequined gown, it went down to 34 percent. She shouldn't have to do the walk of shame.

"Good morning," I said, pulling out the tray of bacon.

"Jesus, what are you making?"

"Breakfast."

She looked over the counter where the toast was buttered and the eggs were piled and ready in the pan. She seemed more disconcerted than anything.

"You all right?"

"Yeah, I just didn't think I was staying for all this."

"You're not hungry?"

"I am."

"You don't like eggs? Or bacon? Or pancakes?"

"I like all that."

"You have somewhere to go?"

"Not really." She sat on the barstool opposite me.

"So, it's me?"

"No."

"I can accept if it's me, you know."

"It's you."

What? I gave her hours' worth of orgasms and told her the absolute truth of how beautiful she was. What else could I do?

"Well." I put down my fork. "I have nothing left."

"That's it? Nothing?"

"I have no more charms."

She leaned over the counter and picked up a piece of bacon, smiling.

"That sucks." She bit the end off and chewed. "Maybe I'll stay for breakfast anyway."

"That's the spirit. Get some plates, would you?"

She got up and came around to my side. Her underwear had gotten shredded the night before, and I became hyperaware that she was naked under her evening dress.

Yeah, I got hard.

"What are you looking at?" she asked as she got two dishes down.

"Your ass. Why?"

"Are you going to look at me like that at work?"

"Probably not."

She put the plates on the counter and looked down pensively.

"This was a mistake."

"Whoa, there—"

"I'm not blaming you, but it's going to be even harder now. And it was already really hard." She was as good as admitting I didn't hold some unrequited attraction to her and she knew it. "Okay, just so you know, yes. I thought you were hot the entire time. From the first minute. But I have a history, and I don't want you to think I'm a slut or something but you might. And if you do, it says more about you than it does about me."

I turned the heat off and scraped eggs onto the plates. "Go on, slut."

She pinched me. It was cute. She was cute. Everything about her was fun.

"Seriously," I said. "Go on."

"I had a thing with my last boss, and it was nothing. Less than nothing and it was fine. But I felt weird at the office and I felt like everyone was talking about me. I don't want that again. I just want this job to be normal, and I don't want to lose it over this."

"So, state explicitly. Do you want to continue with this thing we started? Or not?"

Her mouth tightened and she took a deep breath through her nose before speaking.

"What do you want?"

"Me?" I picked up the plates. I wanted her, but I didn't know what to do about it. "I want to eat breakfast and fuck you again."

"That's not an answer."

"It's the only one I have. Come on. It's Saturday. We're not in the office. Let's just have the weekend to do whatever we want and we'll cross that bridge when we come to it. Or not. But I'm hungry."

I went to the table and put the food down. She tapped her fingers on the counter a few times and then sat in the chair I held out for her.

"You're a little too convincing," she said.

"I'm a lawyer. It's what I do."

She stacked pancake and egg together on her fork, eating it all in a bite.

"You know what's funny? I'm sitting here eating breakfast and I have no idea where I am."

"San Jose." I opened the curtain. "I know it doesn't look it from here."

"Wow, you found a quiet block. Which park is that?"

"Rose Garden."

"Is that the one with the big chess set?"

"Yeah."

"Oh!" She wiggled in her seat while stabbing pancakes and eggs.

"You play?"

"Let's go before the kids take it over. What time is it? What time do they put the pieces out?"

Her voice dropped at the last word when she looked at herself in her evening gown.

"Teagan has things here. Eat up and let's go before the chess club descends."

Chapter 13

RAVEN

I was terrible at chess, but I loved playing. I especially loved the big chess sets because they were so physical.

Roman had tried to get me in bed again, but I shooed him in the shower and by the time he was out I was wearing his sister's clothes with my bronze stilettos from the night before. Apparently, this wasn't a deal breaker.

"I never thought I'd find leggings and a hoodie so fucking hot," he said as he got his hands under the Google pullover.

"It's nine-fifteen already. Come on!"

I pulled him out the door. We crossed the street together. I'd never seen him in weekend gear before, but he looked just as powerful and confident in jeans and a polo shirt as he did in a custom suit. When he looked at me the way he did, I melted as quickly as I did when he was in the office.

"What do I get if I beat you?" he asked when we got to the gate.

"Mmm... I'll buy you dinner?"

"I can buy my own dinner. I was thinking something a little more satisfying. Nutritionally."

"For you or me?"

"You." His smirk told the entire story of how he was going to deliver the nutrients. I was all for it, personally. I wasn't a spitter or a quitter.

"You're so considerate." I was practically purring at that point. "What if I win?"

"Dinner, since you seem so hungry."

"Deal."

Since I hadn't worn the high heels more than a couple of hours the night before, my feet didn't hurt, but when we got to the edge of the park, I stopped short. We had to cross a grassy field. The heels were going to be a problem. I bent a knee and grabbed a heel to take it off.

My first assumption was that I'd lost my balance, because I felt the ground go out from under me. By the time I realized Roman was picking me up and carrying me, I'd hit him in the face trying to get my balance.

"You're a tough cookie." He shifted my weight in his arms, getting comfortable. I put my arms around his neck as he crossed the field.

"You should warn a girl if you're going to pick her up and carry her."

"As if you'd let me."

I kissed his cheek. He hadn't shaved, and his stubble tickled my nose. Without cologne or aftershave, but clean and fresh, he smelled like morning dew.

"Tell me something," I said.

"Something."

"Why aren't you taken?"

"Right now, I'm taken with you."

"I mean it."

He bounced as he carried me, his hair taken by the wind.

"I don't know, honestly." He looked at me, still walking. "I had a girlfriend for a while. Right out of college. But she and I just didn't see eye to eye on a few key issues."

"Such as?"

He stepped onto pavement and lowered me gently. We were by the rec center, the playground, the waterpark that ran in the summer months. The chessboard was just past the swing set. A man in blue coveralls walked out of the shed carrying a black pawn under each arm.

"I was twenty-six," Roman said. "I was different back then."

I could guess what was different. He was a cheater, or a partier, or emotionally lazy. But I wanted him to say it. So I waited. I didn't move toward the chessboard, but didn't put words in his mouth either.

"She wanted to settle down and I wanted to make partner."

"You can't walk and chew gum at the same time?"

"I can. But not with her. And before you ask... There was nothing wrong with her. Or me. It just wasn't happening. Can we talk about something else now? Like how long it's going to take me to checkmate you?"

"Never!" I ran to the chessboard in my heels just as the coverall guy was putting the last pawn in place.

Chapter 14

ROMAN

I had her checkmated in four moves. We went best two out of three and she won a grueling second match. When she picked up the big pieces her hoodie hiked up and I could see her belly. When she kneeled down to pick up a pawn, her feet arched in her high heels with the most feminine curve I'd ever seen.

But the best part was watching her move between the pieces, thinking. Her eyes went from square to square, checking corners and seeing options. Playing the big chess set in the park was like opening up her mind and watching the gears turn.

"Have you ever done any climbing?" I asked, moving my bishop three spaces.

"Like what?" Her hair swung as she traced a line from the bishop I'd moved to the queen I was making a plan to capture. "Like mountains?"

"Yeah. Or rocks."

"I've climbed trees. But not recently." She moved her queen one space. "Check."

"What?"

She pointed. My bishop had been protecting my king. When I'd moved it, she'd been ready.

A small girl with chocolate skin and a heart-printed down jacket stood on the edge of the board with her arms crossed, tapping her light-up sneaker. She looked to be about seven.

"Are you guys done yet?"

As if woken from a spell, I noticed the park had filled up. Kids yelped and squealed. The swings squeaked. The sun burned bright but not hot.

Raven had her hands on her hips. I thought she was going to yell at the kid for interrupting. I didn't want her to. I hadn't told the entire truth about my ex. She'd wanted to settle down, but she didn't like kids. Nothing was less attractive than someone who wasn't nice to children.

"He's in trouble." She pointed to me. "He's in check, and as you can see"—she held her hand out to the board—"he's dead meat in five moves. If you get him out of it, we'll leave."

"Five moves?" the girl said. "He's got you in four!" She jumped onto the board and put her arms around a rook.

"Wait a minute!" Another little voice called from behind me. A boy this time. About the same age as my new partner. "If you move that he can't castle, and she's got him on en-eff-three."

The girl put the rook down and stood next to the boy, looking the board over. I stood next to Raven and said softly, "Is this age appropriate?"

"This is what happens in a city full of geniuses."

"En-eff-three," the girl said. "En-see-six."

"What are they even talking about?" I asked.

"I have no idea." She leaned against me, and I put my arm around her.

The little girl moved my knight in front of my king.

"If we left," I asked, "would they notice?"

"Half-half in six!" the boy cried.

"No." The little girl was offended by the idea. "I can win in four."

I took Raven's hand and led her back the way we came.

"Let's say we both won."

When we got to the edge of the pavement, where the soft grass began, I held my arms out. "Ready?"

"I have a better idea." She took me by the shoulders and turned me. "Piggyback, ready?"

"Ready."

She jumped on my back. I grabbed her calves and started running across the field where a soccer game was in full swing. I kicked the ball, dodged players, and jumped over a rock that would have sent us both flying.

We didn't stop laughing until we tumbled into bed.

Chapter 15

RAVEN

The Russian agent came out of nowhere. He had on a suit and tie. A dapper little fuck with the motherland's flag pinned to his lapel. I pulled the trigger. Missed. He had Roman in a chokehold. They were moving so fast, and I risked shooting Roman instead of the agent, but I had to gamble. I shot. Commie blood splattered everywhere.

"Thank you!" Roman said from next to me.

"I owe you one from the Mauritian Islands mission." I blasted through a line of guys. "Give me cover, I'm—"

"What's that smell?"

Beer and farts would have been my answer five minutes before. The basement of the video-game-themed restaurant reeked of men triggering dopamine responses, which I totally empathized with, because there were things I didn't want to think about right then, either. Space was bought by the hour, not including food. For that you could play whatever video game you wanted either with a friend, a stranger who put their name on the board, or alone without anyone bothering you. The waitresses were specifically instructed to leave the food and go away.

Ours had left a burger, a chicken sandwich, and fries on the table between us, and the smell cut through the stale air.

I snapped my rifle back into the mount. My head was

immediately blown off.

"Damn Russians! Take that!" Roman greased the guy who shot me and put his own gun down. "Vengeance is sweet." He turned his chair to the little table and kissed me. "You should play with Teagan some time. She's a real assassin."

"You keep saying stuff like that."

"Like what?" He bit into his burger as if he didn't have a single thing on his mind.

"Like, 'oh, at some future date this or that should happen.'"

"Mm-hm?" He picked up his glass, pushed the straw out of the way, and washed down his burger with his Coke.

"It's Sunday night."

"So?" He put his glass down and picked his burger up again. I picked up a fry. My appetite for a shitty chicken sandwich had gotten shot out of frame.

"So we're in the office tomorrow. Together. And this was a weekend-only deal. Remember?"

He took another bite, which was completely infuriating. One, it delayed his answer while he chewed. Two, how could he eat at a time like this?

"I mean, I guess I should just appreciate it," I said as much to myself as to him, "but you'll excuse me if I'm not exactly jumping for joy."

He grunted around his burger again. I threw down my French fry.

"We're going to go back to your place," I continued, "fuck a few times, and then what? You dropping me home tonight or tomorrow morning? And how am I supposed to feel? Well, I know what I'm supposed to feel. I'm supposed to feel nothing. But, duh to no one but me, I couldn't have spent an entire weekend with you if I felt nothing." I paused. Roman was looking at me in shock. He'd stopped chewing, but his mouth was still full. I shoved my tray away. "Obviously, you don't have any feelings about it."

I walked out. He could pay the fucking bill. I couldn't look at him.

I didn't know where my fury came from. Maybe from built-up aggression related to not being able to have a relationship outside work when the only men I ever met were at the office. Maybe it was from serial disappointments over everything. Maybe the fact that this stable forever job was turning out to be unstable in a completely different way.

Maybe I just wanted him to like me as much as I liked him.

I jabbed at my phone, walking fast so I could get as far away from the video game restaurant as possible. I'd have the Lyft driver meet me at the next corner, once I got past all the bars on Santa Clara St.

He was a test. He was a test of my commitment to my goals.

Goal number one. Stability.

Men came and went. Sex could be had for the asking. But a stable job was all I ever wanted and it was all I ever risked.

"Jesus." Roman's voice came from behind me. His hands were on his knees and he was out of breath. "You run...so fast...paid bill and..." He pointed back the way we'd come. "Thought you'd...toward Market but..."

I would have run again but the car was meeting me on that corner.

"Roman."

"Wait." He straightened up, arms out. "You did all the talking."

The light across Almaden changed and packs of people crossed, getting between us. We were shoved and separated. I went through to meet him off the corner, in a little patch of empty concrete.

"You're right," I said with the intention of doing even more of the talking. "You saved me from a stupid decision. It was a weekend for a reason. I'm sorry. I lost my priorities for a minute. I like you but I'm not losing my job over you."

A black Kia with a light in the windshield pulled up and rolled down the window.

"Yeah...no." Roman said. "I had food in my mouth. That's not what I was trying to say."

"Raven?" the Kia driver called. She was blocking traffic.

"My Lyft's here."

"Do you really think I'm going to turn into a pumpkin at midnight?"

I opened the door. "The chariot turned into a pumpkin, not the prince."

I got in and closed the door. Roman leapt up and stuck his head in the front window, where the driver had called out.

"I'll see you tomorrow, and I'll know what's under your suit."

"I'll know what's under yours, too. But it won't matter."

He winked at me, the little shit. He was wearing a Henley, but that wink was all tailored suit and French cuffs. It was shiny shoes and expensive cologne. That wink was the confidence that I'd see him on Monday and fall into his arms.

Well, he and his stupid ego-holeness were in for a big surprise.

Chapter 16

ROMAN

Raven ignored me on Monday. She wore a tweed shirt and jacket with a turtleneck, low brown pumps, and her hair in a tortoiseshell headband. She looked as if she was de-sexing herself for my benefit. It didn't work. I knew what her underwear looked like and what her pussy tasted like. I knew how filthy her mouth was and how smooth her skin was.

I'd known the weekend deadline wouldn't stick if I didn't want it to. I was generally very capable of walking away from flings. I didn't make attachments I didn't need to make.

But she was different.

I didn't need to get attached to her, but I hadn't had a choice either. She was like an orange with a tough, attractive skin. Once peeled, she was soft, sticky, sweet.

I was in the middle of a fantasy that involved feeding Raven orange wedges when Marie came in without knocking.

"Ready?"

"Yeah." I snapped out of it. "I've never been up to Burke's new office."

"It's a trip," she said on her way out. I got my things and joined Marie in the hall. As I walked out with her, Raven came down the hall in her sexless pumps. I ignored her, or at least I thought I did. When I looked back toward Marie, I found her watching me suspiciously.

We got into the elevator. I pressed the button to the top floor, Alexander Burke's office suite. The doors closed before anyone else could join us.

"Burke's doing a big event the Friday before rollout. If it's not live on Monday, he's going to be embarrassed. We don't embarrass clients."

"The system will protect Neuronet from some litigation. Performance benchmarks for the sales unit are a little aggressive. They're working on the—"

"Tell me how invaluable you are."

"He's not going to get sued. That's invaluable."

The elevator stopped and opened into a vast room surrounded with windows. It had been designed as another stark, angular office for a Silicon Valley tycoon, but Burke had managed to subvert the original intent. There were stacks of papers everywhere. Crowded corkboards leaning against the wet bar and the bottoms of the windows. The conference table had been turned upside down, and colored yarn had been strung between the six legs like an extreme game of cat's cradle. Post-its with numbers and symbols were clipped to the yarn.

"Captain Kill!" Alexander Burke called in his British accent, coming out from behind a six-foot-tall Lego model of DNA. He had on a black mock-neck tee, a black jacket, and black pants. His socks were Kelly green.

"Bushwhacker!" Calling each other by our gamer names, we gave each other a back-slapping man hug. I hadn't seen my old friend since he'd hired me two months before. He'd been ballooning around Antarctica.

"Marie, right?" He shook her hand. "Perry set up the terrace; it's a mess in here." He walked across the room without looking back at his guests, head bowed as if the world outside his brain was too distracting.

We went out to the terrace overlooking the bay. The inner workings of Burke's mind hadn't spilled out, so it was clean and neat. Drinks had been set out.

"Am I getting my system?" he asked, running his fingers

through his hair again. "I made it simple."

"The software infrastructure was easy. We just worked on the methods."

"My new VP of HR."

"Yes, I worked with her."

"She was at QI4, you know. Hard to get. Very smart."

"Very," I said, about to launch into Raven's virtues.

"She worries me." Marie put her glass down and leaned on the railing. Raven had just left me standing on a street corner the night before, but I still wanted to push her over the edge.

"Really?" Burke asked. "How so?"

"She and Taylor Harden had a thing at her last job."

I had to turn away before I told her to shut the fuck up.

"I heard rumors." Burke shrugged and brought his iced tea to his lips. "But what I wanted to talk to you about was some good news." He put his iced tea on the glass tabletop and picked up an envelope. "Thank you," he said, handing Marie the envelope. "Your team got this done well and on time."

Marie paused, glanced at me to see if I knew what was going on, and seeing I had no fucking clue, she opened the envelope. I couldn't see it from where I stood, but the sun shone through it enough for me to discern both the check and her stunned reaction to it.

"We haven't billed yet," she said.

"That's a bonus on top of billing. To thank you guys for getting it done."

Burke didn't know what Marie wanted or how badly she wanted it, so he didn't sense that her gratitude was genuine and grudging at the same time.

"If you're hiring new outside counsel for future projects—"

"I'm thinking of keeping it in-house for now."

She put the check back in the envelope and folded the flap back. She was a wild card.

"It's been a pleasure, Alex," I said, hoping to end this and get out, because Marie had had her eyes on a single target from jump, and it was a target I wanted to protect. "Really great. Any time you—"

"Our job is to protect our client from lawsuits," Marie cut in. "Be the eyes and ears of the world outside Neuronet."

"Of course."

"I think you need that." She glanced at me, then back at Burke. Her gears were turning. "So if you ever feel isolated, or like you need ears on the ground, let us know."

She picked up her glass. I had the feeling my name wasn't getting put on the stationery this time around.

* * * *

In the elevator, on the way down, we watched the numbers change.

"You're having a thing with Raven Crosby."

Marie stated it as a fact. I swallowed a vigorous denial. The question needed a question.

"What makes you say that?"

"What makes you not deny it?"

I didn't answer. The elevator slowed and stopped.

"I'll keep an eye on her," I said as the doors opened. "But if there's nothing there, there's nothing there. I'm not going to invent suspicion to look useful."

"Agreed."

I walked out of the elevator with the best of intentions, but once I got to my office and saw her across from me, I wasn't sure if I was going to make it.

Chapter 17

RAVEN

"Wait," Masy said, glancing at me from the TV. She had a bowl of popcorn in her lap, ready for her Friday night show. "So you came home right after on Sunday out of spite, and you're still ignoring him out of spite."

"I'm ignoring him out of necessity."

Since I'd gotten into a car without him five days before, we'd had two in-office meetings. I thought he'd try to get under my skirt or make innuendos. I thought he'd send an email or a note, but no. Nothing. He was a model of professionalism.

I was glad he respected my wishes, but I was also disappointed. It was hard to sit across a table from him when his cologne was such sweet citrus. My father used a citrus scented brush cleaner, and it reminded me of when he'd let me paint. The creativity of childhood. The freedom of the instability.

I wanted him to look at me, but he barely did. I wanted his eyes to peel me down to the underwear he knew I was wearing. I wanted to feel naked and exposed with him, but he'd put a wall between us and I had to admit, I did too. My desire bounced off it, back at me. By Friday I'd given myself an unsatisfying orgasm every single night.

"Are you watching *Empire* with me?" Masy folded her legs under her.

"I'm going to the gym. I'll watch it on the treadmill and we can discuss." I needed to work Roman out of my muscles. I was looking forward to beating the hell out of them until I was too exhausted to fall asleep thinking about him.

* * * *

Twenty minutes into the treadmill, I was at a full canter, really close to that state of blissful concentration that excluded everything else. Close, because I was still aroused thinking about Roman. He wouldn't get out of my mind. He was tenacious, hanging onto my thoughts whenever I became aware of my body. The blister on my heel, the burning breaths, the sweat dripping down my neck, my nails digging into my palm.

Someone had on his lemony cologne. I could turn up my headphones and I could even close my eyes if I saw something I didn't want to see. But I couldn't stop *breathing*. I increased the incline and turned up the sound on *Empire*.

He'd been such a surprise. Sexy and powerful, just the way I liked my men, but what that scent brought back was the fact that he was so much fun. He joked. He played. He made me smile. I stopped trying to avoid thoughts of him and let them come. The color of his hair and his gray-green eyes that I realized were the exact color of artichokes. His smile. His spontaneity. His stupid jokes and his terribly clever ones.

I realized I was smiling and looked up at myself in the mirror.

There was the source of the cologne. Roman was running on the treadmill next to me. He made the peace sign in the mirror.

I punched the stop button and the treadmill came to an abrupt halt. I hopped off and snapped my towel off the rail.

"That's weird, Roman. Just weird."

He calmly stopped his treadmill. My clothes and hair stuck to me and I was breathing like a dog. No man should see me like that, but this man in particular had no choice.

"I'm a member, Raven. Since way before I met you."

"You just stood there watching me."

"I wasn't standing. I was running." He wiped his face with his towel, not that he needed to. Even sweaty, he was perfect.

"Seriously? That's your excuse?" My voice was raised a notch.

He shrugged and smiled a little.

"Can you avoid me outside the office too, please? Or tell me when you're next to me like a normal person?"

"I avoided you all week."

"You suck at it."

He looked as if he was about to answer with some kind of unacceptable wisecrack when a male voice came from my left.

"Miss?" It was a security guard.

"Yes?"

"I'm sorry, is this gentleman bothering you?"

I glanced at Roman, then back to the security guard, who was undoubtedly doing exactly the job he'd been hired to do. This forced me to ask myself whether or not I was going to talk to Roman. I thought I'd have a minute more to decide.

"No," I said. "He's a friend of mine. But thanks."

"Keep it down, then."

"We will." I shot him a look, but he just smiled.

The guard nodded and walked back to the door. Screw this. I stormed toward the locker room, knowing he was right behind me.

Maybe I didn't storm.

If I'd wanted Roman to go away, I'd storm off and slam the door behind me, cutting him off. But he was following me, I knew it, and I was happy about it. By the time I got to the locker rooms, I slowed down so he could catch up.

"What do you want?" I hissed, even though I wasn't mad. I had an act to keep up.

"I want to talk to you."

"About what?"

"How's this week been for you, Raven?"

"Honestly?"

"Honestly."

"You really want to know?"

"I do. I want to know if you feel like you're being pulled toward me whenever we pass in the hall. I want to know how much effort it takes for you to not look through those office windows.

How many draft emails you've deleted. Because, me? I've tried. I've tried to stop thinking about you. I've tried to stop wanting you. I fail. I've completely failed, and I need to know that either you've failed too, or I want you to tell me how you did it."

I took a deep breath. I knew I could lie. I could say I just didn't give enough of a crap to have to do anything. I never thought about him. Didn't want him. Wanted nothing to do with him outside work.

"Last night," I said, "I swore I was never going to think of you again. But there I was, lying in bed, and I thought about you. So I did the same thing I did every other night this week." A woman came out of the locker room, and I dropped my voice. "I put my hand between my legs and fingered myself until I could hear your voice and feel your cock stretching me open. When I came, I said your name." Our faces inched closer. "Roman." His breath was on my lips. "Roman."

Our lips touched and one last time, I said, "Roman."

He stood up straight. "Not here. We're five blocks from the office. God, I'm an idiot when I'm near you." He pushed open the door behind me. It was a private, unisex bathroom. I fell backward into it.

The motion sensor lights buzzed on.

He snapped the lock.

"We have to talk about this," I said.

He picked me up under my arms and sat me on the vanity.

"Let's talk. First of all,"—he opened my legs, exposing the wet patch between them—"we go on the down low. We kept our pants on all week. We keep doing that. We know we can."

"Second," I said, pulling his waistband down and getting his dick out. "This is not casual. If it's casual for you, forget it."

He groaned when I rubbed his cock, but nodded. "Not casual."

"Good."

He took my waistband and pulled it down. I raised my bottom so he could slide the pants to my knees. He knocked a shoe off and unpeeled one pant leg.

"If we get caught," he said, sliding the head over my wetness, "it's on me. I cover for you however I see fit."

"We can both take the—" He entered me and I arched into him. "We can both, oh…yes."

"Yes?" He went harder when he asked, and my mind shattered into a thoughtless burst of agreement.

"Yes, yes."

He licked his thumb and rubbed my clit in the rhythm of our thrusts. I clutched his shirt, leveraging myself against him as he held me on the vanity so I wouldn't fall when I came. I bit back a scream and let my throat rattle with my orgasm. He came inside me a second after, leaving his handprint on the mirror.

"Say you're mine," he whispered in my ear. I took his face in my hands.

"I'm yours, but how long can we do this?"

"Until Siska and Welton's contract is up. Three weeks."

"So soon?"

"I can neither confirm nor deny our contract is being renewed. But in three weeks, we'll have a little elbow room."

My body was still wrapped around his on the counter of a public bathroom, but inside I was exploding with joy.

"Can you make it?" I asked, because I wasn't sure if I could.

"Keep wearing those brown shoes and I might."

Chapter 18

ROMAN

It sounded crazy. The idea that I'd sit with Marie and discuss keeping an eye out to see if Raven was screwing an employee, then becoming that employee.

Who would do that?

I figured it this way. If the employee was *me*, she was safe. I wouldn't rat her out. I'd protect her. I'd make sure if she needed to satisfy that insane sexual appetite with someone, it would be a guy who respected her and would keep it quiet.

Me, me, me.

It was as if I was on some kind of reality-altering drug that made the most insane shit seem perfectly reasonable. If you took a wire O and twisted it enough, it became an 8. Same O, also an 8, well within the bounds of reality if you just bent your mind a bit.

And if you wanted that 8 so badly you'd twist an O made of steel rebar? Which was at least as much as I wanted Raven? Then you pumped up the muscles of your brain until you twisted that shit all around.

And that was exactly what I did.

I made sense from nonsense. Real from fantasy. I spent the weekend with her, made her meals because I couldn't take her out, had her body in every room of the house. I didn't feel an ounce of guilt or shame for not telling her what Marie had said, because frankly, I was gone in three weeks. Out. We just had to hold it together for that long. Wait maybe another month, then we could be normal. Eat out. Go to events. All of it.

"Two more weekends," she said as I walked her to my driveway. She counted down the days the same way I was about to.

"Right after launch," I said, pinning her to the side of her Audi. I couldn't stop kissing her. It had become a habit, a check-in from my lips to hers, as if they needed to make sure, minute to minute, that she was there. "I'm back to my office and you are in my bed."

"You can stay at my house for a change."

"Where do you live again?"

"Somewhere around. I forget."

I couldn't keep off her. I didn't know how I was going to let her get in the car.

"Stay here tonight. We'll get up at four and you can go home for clothes."

"I'll be late."

"You won't be late."

She pushed me away and put her finger up in front of my face.

"You, sir, are a lawyer. You can work anywhere. I love this job and I want to keep it. So, no, I cannot risk being late. Not even five minutes."

She gave me another little push, then pulled me close. I gave her a kiss. A serious good-bye kiss that meant I was letting her get in the car, finally, once and for all, immediately, if not sooner. Once I was done kissing her.

"Go!" I said, pulling away. "Before I bend you over this car."

"Tempting." She popped the door open.

"Don't dare me."

"I'm not." She slid in and closed the door. She already seemed too far away. I rapped on the window. She started the engine and rolled down the window.

"What are you wearing under your sensible little suit tomorrow?" I asked.

She thought for a second, then let a sly grin spread across her face.

"White lace."

She took off before I could tell her that was my favorite.

Chapter 19

RAVEN

Whether Roman was in proximity or not, I felt a disconnection between one part of my life and the others. My life had been contained, neat, manageable. After I met him the lid came unscrewed and the contents spilled out. I had to walk around the office like a normal person, but I felt like I was leaving breadcrumbs behind. Emotions I couldn't contain. Bits of sadness and longing. Nuggets of happiness and satisfaction like brightly colored stones leading back to a house I'd never seen before. So thick was the disorientation that I questioned every word I said as if someone else was being so damn professional when I felt as if every solid thing in my body was turning molten. I took lunch at my desk so I could avoid a conversation about my social life. I had no idea what I'd blurt out, or if my eyes would give me away. My reluctance to say anything could be a signal. For at least three weeks, I needed to pretend the lid was on the jar.

We were great. We said hello and good-bye. Please and thank you. When the system had an issue and we happened to meet in the hall, we talked about the system and nothing else. We stayed a respectful distance apart, and though our bodies didn't touch, neither one of us could control our eyes. His sought out a bra strap or garter line. Mine looked at his lips and his hands. The shape of them. The way they moved. His dick was safely put away, but the lips and hands had touched me. My nipples got hard and my panties got wet. I didn't go to the executive bathroom and release the tension. I saved it for him.

We complimented each other's professionalism every weeknight, lying in separate towns, separate houses, separate beds.

—What time did you leave?—

We asked this every night. Even if I saw him walk out the door, I asked.

—*Seven-thirty. You?*—
—Still here. I had a dinner with a new associate—
—*Where?*—
—Bird Dog. But all I wanted to eat was you—

That was how it began. A soft segue from the office talk to us talk. If one of us was in the office, we'd text. If we were both home, we'd call.

—Are you alone?—

Masy had gone out with some mutual friends. I could have joined her, but then I would have missed the highlight of my nights. Roman.

—*Yes*—

I touched the gray dots at the bottom, waiting for his reply. It was washed into black when the phone rang. It was him.

"Hi," I said. I heard a door click on the other side.

"I'm not in the mood for autocorrect. And I want to hear you."

"Hear me what?"

"Describe your apartment."

I flopped on the couch. He'd never been over, so it was a legitimate question, even if it was a waste of time.

"I'm on the bottom floor. It's one big room. Kitchen attached to living room with an island in between."

"Doors and windows?"

"On either side. Front and back. Front has a porch onto the street, back goes to a courtyard."

I heard his fingers drum on the desk and the clack of keys.

"What are you doing?" I asked.

"Working. Keep going. What do you have in there that's yours? I don't want to hear what the architect decided."

What could I talk about? The rocking chair we pulled off the curb? The basket of laundry I had to fold? The coffeemaker my mother bought me when I moved in?

"My dress for the release gala is hanging over the bannister."

"What's it look like?"

"It's a halter top. The top part is beaded in a dark silver color."

"Touch it."

I was taken aback for a second. I'd been getting comfortable on the couch and collecting adjectives for the dress. But Roman was always a good phone partner, so I got up and put my hands on the beaded bodice.

"What's it feel like?" he asked.

"Like beads and lace."

"I want to know what my hands are going to feel when I pull it off you."

I took a deep breath as my glands shot arousal hormones into my blood. Running my hand over the top of the dress, the beads shifted and rolled under my fingers, while the threads caught in my nails.

"It's rough," I said. "And delicate. But the lace is soft."

"Are you wet?" he whispered into the phone. "Check." I imagined him with the door closed and the blinds shut, whispering against late-night interlopers as I slid my hand below my waistband. I was wet and open, throbbing when my finger touched my hard nub.

"Yeah. I'm wet."

"Keep your hand there. Tell me about the bottom of the dress. More beads?"

"Tulle. Silver gray."

"What am I going to feel when I put my hand up it? Feel it, and feel yourself with your other hand."

I tucked the phone between my ear and my shoulder and got my clean hand up the dress.

"Soft. Silk lining."

He gasped hard. "Take a handful."

"Are you...?"

"Yes." He said it with a groan.

He was jerking off under the desk. All the times I'd seen him in that office and wanted him to fuck me, he was jerking off for me right there. Such a turn-on.

"It's scratchy when you rub it together," I said. "The tulle has traction when you grab it but the silk lining slides." I couldn't think of anything else to say about the dress. "I got stockings. Since it's a long dress, I'm not wearing panties. Just a garter. Silver-gray lace. You can have your thumb under the strap and a finger inside me."

I moved my finger off my clit and put it inside, closing around it so I could feel every bit of pressure.

"You're so dirty."

"I'm going to come soon."

"Say my name."

I almost lost the phone when I did, running two fingers along my seam, half standing, half crouching with a fistful of satin and tulle in my other hand.

"Roman."

"Say you're mine."

"I'm yours, I am yours. So yours."

"Damn right."

I came leaning against the bannister. The phone dropped to the carpet. My back arched and the rest of my body followed until my toes held my weight and my mind went utterly blank. I let go of the dress and sat on the bottom step. My hand was soaked with my juices, so I put it palm up on my knee. Roman would lick it clean.

"Hey," I said, snapping the phone up.

"Thanks for that."

"You came at your desk?"

"Under it, into a napkin from lunch."

"That's so hot and sexy." Shifting sideways on the step, I leaned on the wall and put my feet on the bannister rail. My dress hung on the other side. I'd have to steam the wrinkles out before Friday, then Roman would crumple it again.

"Were you serious about the underwear?"

"Yep. I have it but I'm not wearing it."

He paused. I didn't know if he was zipping up or what. Maybe he was turned on again.

"Wear it. Please."

"Why?"

"Because the idea of you being in public without it bothers me. It makes me want to cover you. I don't know why. Maybe I'm being protective."

"I swear this dress is to the floor."

"I know. I'm not saying I'm making sense, but if you're leaving them off for me, you can put them on for me."

"You're being really bossy."

"Yeah. And I'm sorry, but I'm not. You can boss me about something that's important to you some time."

"Hm. How about next time I'm over we play *Destiny 2* instead of *Call of Duty?*"

"Fair trade."

"Good."

"I have to go or I'm going to be here all night."

"Okay."

I never understood the "you hang up first," "no, you hang up" meme. Now I did. I floundered because I wanted to cap off the conversation with "I love you," but we weren't ready. Not until he left the Neuronet office.

We hung up and I held the phone to my chest.

I did love him.

Chapter 20

ROMAN

The Neuronet campus courtyard was set up for events up to a thousand people, and the company took advantage whenever possible. The doors to the indoor space folded out, opening up the entire wall to the courtyard. The circular steps made concrete bleachers. The fountain was lit with color-changing lights.

I had a silver tie to match the dress I hadn't seen. I'd gotten pretty close with the color, but I couldn't match her radiance. She didn't drink at work socials, but kept a glass of water in her hand as she greeted Everett Fitzgerald and Alexander Burke, tech giants showing up for another on-campus party.

Raven was almost mine. I'd approved the system, along with my entire team and the HR department. If Neuronet got sued or had a PR debacle over compensation, it wouldn't be over the system. I'd packed up my office supplies like a kid moving to a different room in the house. Sure, I was just moving back to my old office across the bay, but everything outside that was changing for the better.

"Why are you smiling?" Marie asked, sidling up to me. "You're like a cat with a pillow full of canary feathers."

"I like finishing things." I held up my glass and she clinked it.

"Well, that's sweet, but I have good news."

"I like good news."

Raven was nodding to Fitz. She knew him from QI4. Seeing her with a tall, young guy who had more money than God made me want to go over there and kiss her. Just to make sure every multi-billion-dollar mogul knew they had to look elsewhere.

"Good news is, Burke renewed the contract."

My attention snapped away from Raven to my boss.

"Excuse me?"

Over Marie's shoulder I saw Raven and Fitz with another man. Taylor Harden.

The first thing I thought of was her underwear. She'd promised to wear all the pieces in the set, but what if she decided to surprise me? What if there was only a couple of loose layers of silk between her and her old flame?

Taylor laughed at something.

That bothered me, mostly because she was having a conversation with him, a relationship, and I couldn't go near her.

I shook it off. Barely.

"It was quite a sell, but I told them the only way to make sure the new VP is on the up and up is to throw a little temptation her way."

I couldn't unravel that while Taylor put his hand on Raven's arm. It was a friendly gesture that could be explained away, but I was a stew of shit and foulness at that moment.

Marie winked at me and sipped her champagne.

"What?"

"Don't worry. You earned yourself a name on the door."

"By doing what?"

"What handsome men do. We got the contract renewed. We'll be handling risk management and executive vetting. And the retainer fee? Very nice. You'll have an office right below Burke at the General Counsel."

"Hold on. Just let me say this back to you. I was supposed to have a thing with Raven?"

"You were supposed to test her," Marie said. "She failed. You're safe. And in the meantime your team put together a system the client can be confident in. Why do you look like that? Are you all right?"

"You used me as a honey trap?"

"I wouldn't call us Siska, Welton + Bianchi unless you were also an excellent lawyer."

Great.

I was an excellent lawyer.

"How did you find out?"

"I took her assistant out for a drink. She saw you two at the symphony."

The SSV. The symphony I never actually saw. The violation got wider and the shame got deeper.

"Are you getting offended?" Marie asked. "If I told you, you would have tried too hard. That wouldn't have been fair."

Was I angry with Marie for using me? For playing me so she could play Raven so she could play Burke? Was I uncomfortable because we'd been so good at keeping our affair under wraps? Yes. All of it.

Did it have nothing to do with being manipulated? Was I disappointed that I had to stay at Neuronet?

None of it.

I was upset that in trying to protect Raven, I'd played right into endangering her dreams. I was the only thing standing between her and what she wanted most. Permanence.

I wanted to be her stability, not her chaos. I'd hurt her. I was regretful, angry, and helpless inside it because I had what I wanted.

I'd destroyed Raven and our relationship in the meantime, and there was not a goddamn thing I could do about it.

"I got my partnership." I put my glass on a waiter's tray. "That was all I wanted."

"Congratulations."

"Thank you. Excuse me for a minute."

I had no patience for the party, but I couldn't stand the idea of going home. I had to think. I went back up to my office.

Chapter 21

RAVEN

At one point, just as I was starting to relax, I felt Roman looking at me. Taylor was talking about some impossible aspect of quantum physics, and his new girlfriend corrected him with a snide remark that made him laugh. I think she corrected him. She could have been agreeing. I had no idea what they were saying, and not because the feeling that Roman was near distracted me. I didn't know enough about quantum computing to make jokes about it.

Looking around, I didn't see him. I wasn't supposed to talk to him at the event, but we hadn't said anything about looking at each other.

Finally, I found him. He was a tall silhouette in a window on the second floor. His old office looked down on the courtyard and he was watching me from above.

I excused myself and went upstairs.

"Hey," I said when I got up there. He had a banker's box on his desk. He took a picture of him and his sister out and laid it behind the computer, where it had always been. "I thought you were packing up."

"I was."

"That looks suspiciously like unpacking."

He took a leather folder out of the box and laid it on the desk, then reached in for something else, ignoring me so pointedly I went from comfortably happy to deflated and awkward in fifteen seconds.

But I didn't press him. I stood there and waited. It was his turn to talk and I had nothing to offer. I assumed he was sad he wouldn't see me every day, or that he'd miss the fun of the secrecy.

"You know," he started. "I went to law school because I wasn't going to make it as a video game designer or player, and I had nothing else going on. But I like it. I like what I do. I like protecting companies from their own stupidity. I like knowing the law and using it to prevent lawsuits. It's not glamorous. But it's what I got, and you want stability, I get it. So do I. I want to be a senior partner so I can bust my ass ten months a year and take the other two up in the Sierras."

He'd invited me up to the Sierras with him, up away from the noise of the city. But this didn't feel like an invitation. It felt like the opposite.

"I have things that are important to me." He put his hands on the edge of the box. "I wanted to make senior partner. I did that."

"That's great!"

I was genuinely happy for him, but something was off. He took a planner out of the box but didn't put it on the desk.

"And we've been retained as outside counsel on risk management."

"Ah." So that was it. He wasn't leaving the company. He was going to be around and as a couple, we were screwed. "That's—"

"Great," he snapped.

"Great, but it's across campus, so—"

"That's got no impact on the fraternization between us."

"No," I said. " I mean I get it but—"

"Which shouldn't have happened in the first place."

"You can stop fucking interrupting me now." I let sharpness cut into my voice. I was done with being treated like crap.

He looked at me for the first time, and that gray green was darkened to steel. Cold, hard steel. I didn't like it.

"What I was trying to say was that you shouldn't be putting all your stuff back on this desk when you'll probably be over in the General Counsel's office."

"Right." He dropped the planner, snapped up the picture and the leather folder and put them back in the box.

"So what do you want to do?" I asked.

He sighed. I'd never heard Roman sigh. He wasn't a resigned kind of person. Or maybe I just didn't know him.

"I don't know."

"You don't know?"

"No. I don't. I was totally unprepared for this."

He was unprepared. Boo-fucking-hoo. I was getting a little pissed off. The bucket was filling, but wasn't quite there yet.

"So, you want to split up?"

"I didn't say that."

"You didn't not say it either."

"If you have a suggestion, I'm all ears."

Bucket. Full.

"I have a suggestion. Yeah. I do. You stop acting like a spineless jackass and decide if you want me or not. Because if you don't, I can move on. And just say it, you don't. If you did, you'd say fuck Neuronet and fuck the firm. I'm with Raven. She's mine and none of this other shit matters. But you didn't. You balked. So I'm sitting here, ready to toss everything and start over for the sake of being with you, and you're rearranging shit in a cardboard box. That tells me everything I need to know about what I mean to you. You should have listened to my email if you were going to do this."

If he was going to argue with me or defend himself, he didn't do it quickly enough. He didn't leap to comfort me or disabuse me of my convictions. He just stood there with his hands in that motherfucking box as the music from the party rose up from the courtyard.

"For your information," I said, "I wore underwear for you."

I spun around before I was even finished, walking down the carpeted hall so fast the tulle flew out behind me. I didn't want to be stuck in an elevator with him, so I took the stairs. The door clapped closed behind me and my shoes clicked on the concrete.

His did not.

The stairway was silent except for my clacking shoes. Every step hurt. The shoes were too high. My toes were jammed and my heels were blistered. That didn't hurt half as much as the realization that he wasn't following me. I was as good as alone in this world. Employed. Safe. Steady and alone.

I didn't have him, but I had this stupid job. Without realizing it, I'd chosen stability over love, and so had he. I hadn't had a warning, time to think, weigh the pros and cons.

That's not how life works, is it? Choices aren't made so clearly by filling in boxes or clicking one button instead of the other. Choices are made over time, little by little while we aren't looking, until the result is inevitable and the consequences are unavoidable.

Stepping onto the courtyard, I slowed down. If the career was what I'd chosen, I wasn't fucking it up by running through the event like a damsel in distress.

I was, however, going to power through my aching feet, go right through the party, and disappear on the other side.

"Raven!" It was fucking Taylor running behind me.

"What?"

"Are you all right?"

"I'm fine."

"Okay, yeah. No."

He took me by the elbow and I jerked away. He put his hands up. Was I making a scene? I didn't want to make a scene.

"I have to—"

"You're crying." He took a hankie out of his pocket and flipped it to me. I touched my cheek. It was wet. For the first time, I noticed my breath was catching.

"Great." I dabbed under my eyes. "Just great."

"If it's the job, you know you can come back to QI4."

He dangled his little treasure in front of me as if I was a kitten and he'd just brought home a new toy. Going back to QI4 would solve the Roman problem, even if that meant I got away from him, but it wouldn't solve the *me* problem.

"What is it with me, Taylor? Why do I end up with guys I work with?"

He shrugged, looking around as if trying to find someone besides himself.

"Not you, asshole. But yeah. You. Plus."

His eyes lit on his new girlfriend, who was talking to Fitz a few feet away.

"There's something about seeing a person doing what they're good at that's sexy. Outside work they're normal. You might not even notice them. But when you see someone where they're important—needed. Competent. Whatever, add your adjective—it's pretty hot."

I laughed a little, just enough for him to hear.

"What?" he asked.

"I never took you for someone who could tell me about myself. But, yeah. I just need to find a company without a non-fraternization policy or something."

"Can you imagine the orgies?"

We laughed together. I sniffed. Dabbed the sides of my nose.

Roman was looking at me from the cafeteria, standing with some of the lawyers who had been in and out of the office and an older red-haired woman in a pants suit.

I was supposed to be going home. I'd told myself I was crossing the courtyard and going down to the parking lot. I was going to rip the damn shoes off and drive like there was no tomorrow.

"I was actually thinking of leaving it out of the QI4 policy," Taylor said from the other end of a very long tunnel.

I needed to do what I was supposed to do. Walk to the parking lot. Immediately. Because Roman was coming toward me with the pantsuit woman in tow, chatting at him as if he was listening.

"...sixteen-hour days, and if we're going to have a bunch of..."

He wasn't. His eyes were on me.

"...coders in the cage, it's going to happen anyway..."

Taylor could tell me his crazy idea another time. I turned and tried to walk away while he was midsentence, crashing right into Burke.

"Whoa!" he cried, rescuing his drink from a major spill.

Taylor, "...why not be a disruptor in...whoa!"

"I'm sorry!"

"It's fine," Burke said, getting his balance. "I was coming here to—"

"Raven," Roman's tone demanded attention but Burke was in the middle of... "—I need to talk to you."

"Okay," I said to Burke, as Roman held up a piece of paper. "We can go over by the Big Circuit," I continued absently as Roman flung the piece of paper at me. I caught it.

"You finally got what you wanted." Roman had the attention of the entire circle. Even Taylor redirected from his radical fraternization policy.

Mr. Bianchi:

Thank you for joining me for lunch.

As a matter for the record, you have pursued me up to the limit I find appropriate.

I didn't need to finish it. I skipped to my name and title at the end.

"I didn't publish this," I said.

"But you sent it." Roman pointed at me as if he wanted to nail me to the wall. The gesture was accusatory and forgiving at the same time.

Marie held her hand out for the page. I gave it to her.

"Yeah," I said. "So?"

"So, I didn't listen. Well, now you have what you want. I'm across the campus. Are you happy now?"

My mouth hung open. I wasn't happy, but somehow I knew I was supposed to play along with an act I hadn't rehearsed.

Marie handed me back the letter. "Mr. Bianchi," she said. "Let's discuss this elsewhere."

"No. You did your job a little too well. You wanted to test her, but I was the one who failed. I'm obsessed with her. She's perfect for me, even if she doesn't know it. Perfect, and being here, looking at her every day? It's been hell, and I can't do it any more."

I was so confused, but that was about to get worse.

"You know what?" He threw his hands up. "I quit."

He walked away without looking back.

FILE UNDER: Free

Chapter 22

RAVEN

I had pieced it all together in the following ten minutes, with my official rejection of the man I loved crunching in my hand, then I got in my car, kicked my uncomfortable shoes off, and drove to him in my stocking feet.

Burke had been about to fire me.

There was no traffic, and the streetlamps streaked by as I broke the speed limit to get to him. My phone was face down on the passenger seat. Out of the corner of my eye, it lit up, bleeding light from the space between the device and the leather. I didn't answer. Dying on the way to him would defeat the purpose.

Oona was raving about the SSV show. She said she saw us in the hall together, not knowing Marie was Roman's boss.

I wasn't sure if my job was completely safe. I wasn't sure if any job was ever completely safe. But it was safe from my love for Roman Bianchi.

When I saw him in the office, he was trapped.

I passed the edge of the park. The grassy field he'd carried me over twice was spotted with dim yellow lights. The chess pieces were put away. Leaves rustled over the board. I parked and took a breath. His car was in the driveway.

He'd made partner, then quit to protect me.

What would we do now?

My feet hurt when I put my heels back on, as if protesting losing their freedom so soon. I left my shawl in the car and went unprotected into the chilly night. As I walked across the street to his front door, I asked myself what I wanted from him. From us. I wanted everything, but he'd given up so much already.

His door opened and he stood in the frame with his jacket and tie gone. He worked on undoing his French cuff while my heels clacked along the walk.

"Ms. Crosby," he said.

"Mr. Bianchi."

We faced each other. He absently slipped his cufflinks in his pocket. I put my hands on my hips.

"I didn't tell you how nice you looked in that underwear," he said.

"You didn't have to quit."

"On the contrary. If I wanted you, I had to. And I want you."

I started to explain that he didn't have to resign. We could have figured it out somehow, but he held his hand out.

"Let me finish."

I crossed my arms impatiently. I hoped he wasn't going to talk all that long. I wanted to kiss him, and soon. But his posture was clear. No kissing. Not yet.

"I could have stayed with you on the down low," he continued. "But that's not a long-term solution, and I want a long-term solution. I could have been assigned outside Neuronet, but that would have damaged my seniority in the firm. I wasn't letting you quit. I wasn't going to let you be fired. I wasn't getting in the way of what you need."

I couldn't bear it. I had to talk.

"But you wanted to make partner."

"True."

"You love your job."

"False," he said. "I enjoy my job. It's you I love."

Did my feet hurt?

Were my arms cold in the spring night?

My eyes. Were they dry? Or did a layer of tears form between me and the sight of him?

"I don't want to hurt you," was all I could choke out before I had to swallow a throat full of sobs.

"You're not hurting me." He broke the threshold and took my bare shoulders in his hands. "The partnership was a brass ring, but when you walked out of my office, I realized I traded a gold ring for brass. You are my ambition. You are my mountain to climb. You're my only aspiration."

I took a step closer and put my hands on his chest. He'd never felt so real and solid as that moment, heavy and hard in my hands. A man of substance.

"What are you going to do?"

"I can hang out my own shingle. Nothing gets respect in this town like a guy striking out on his own."

All that might have been true, but I wasn't ready for it. I met his eyes, nearly clear in the glare of the house lights.

"I'm so sorry."

"Be sorry if you don't want me."

"Oh, Roman—"

"Is that you saying you're sorry?" His thumb wiped a tear from my cheek.

"It's me saying I want you. I'm sorry it came to this, but I love you, and I want you. And thank you." I tried to paint my voice with humility and gratitude, but couldn't meet the depth of what I felt in my heart. "Thank you. I can't thank you enough for changing your life for me."

He brushed my biceps with his fingertips. "You're goosebumpy."

The cold caught up with me. The neat up-do felt like a ton of bricks on my head, and my feet burned at the balls.

"It's chilly." He kissed me gently, his lips an invitation and a promise.

We kissed between words right on his front walk, as if I'd finally seen the light after he'd quit. As if we'd just begun the journey of our lives.

"How about a hot bath?" he said, kissing me again. I didn't know how much longer I could stand.

"My feet are going to love that."

"The rest of you isn't going to complain, either."

His hands slid down my arms and we wove our fingers together. He leaned back and we walked into his house together.

—GAME OVER—

Sign up for the 1001 Dark Nights Newsletter
and be entered to win a Tiffany Key necklace.

There's a contest every month!

Go to www.1001DarkNights.com to subscribe.

As a bonus, all subscribers will receive a free
1001 Dark Nights story
The First Night
by Lexi Blake & M.J. Rose

Discover 1001 Dark Nights Collection Four
Go to www.1001DarkNights.com for more information.

ROCK CHICK REAWAKENING by Kristen Ashley
A Rock Chick Novella

ADORING INK by Carrie Ann Ryan
A Montgomery Ink Novella

SWEET RIVALRY by K. Bromberg

SHADE'S LADY by Joanna Wylde
A Reapers MC Novella

RAZR by Larissa Ione
A Demonica Underworld Novella

ARRANGED by Lexi Blake
A Masters and Mercenaries Novella

TANGLED by Rebecca Zanetti
A Dark Protectors Novella

HOLD ME by J. Kenner
A Stark Ever After Novella

SOMEHOW, SOME WAY by Jennifer Probst
A Billionaire Builders Novella

TOO CLOSE TO CALL by Tessa Bailey
A Romancing the Clarksons Novella

HUNTED by Elisabeth Naughton
An Eternal Guardians Novella

EYES ON YOU by Laura Kaye
A Blasphemy Novella

BLADE by Alexandra Ivy/Laura Wright
A Bayou Heat Novella

DRAGON BURN by Donna Grant
A Dark Kings Novella

TRIPPED OUT by Lorelei James
A Blacktop Cowboys® Novella

STUD FINDER by Lauren Blakely

MIDNIGHT UNLEASHED by Lara Adrian
A Midnight Breed Novella

HALLOW BE THE HAUNT by Heather Graham
A Krewe of Hunters Novella

DIRTY FILTHY FIX by Laurelin Paige
A Fixed Novella

THE BED MATE by Kendall Ryan
A Room Mate Novella

PRINCE ROMAN by CD Reiss

NO RESERVATIONS by Kristen Proby
A Fusion Novella

DAWN OF SURRENDER by Liliana Hart
A MacKenzie Family Novella

Discover 1001 Dark Nights Collection One

Go to www.1001DarkNights.com for more information.

Also from 1001 Dark Nights

Discover 1001 Dark Nights Collection Two

Go to www.1001DarkNights.com for more information.

WICKED WOLF by Carrie Ann Ryan
WHEN IRISH EYES ARE HAUNTING by Heather Graham
EASY WITH YOU by Kristen Proby
MASTER OF FREEDOM by Cherise Sinclair
CARESS OF PLEASURE by Julie Kenner
ADORED by Lexi Blake
HADES by Larissa Ione
RAVAGED by Elisabeth Naughton
DREAM OF YOU by Jennifer L. Armentrout
STRIPPED DOWN by Lorelei James
RAGE/KILLIAN by Alexandra Ivy/Laura Wright
DRAGON KING by Donna Grant
PURE WICKED by Shayla Black
HARD AS STEEL by Laura Kaye
STROKE OF MIDNIGHT by Lara Adrian
ALL HALLOWS EVE by Heather Graham
KISS THE FLAME by Christopher Rice
DARING HER LOVE by Melissa Foster
TEASED by Rebecca Zanetti
THE PROMISE OF SURRENDER by Liliana Hart

Also from 1001 Dark Nights

THE SURRENDER GATE By Christopher Rice
SERVICING THE TARGET By Cherise Sinclair

Discover 1001 Dark Nights Collection Three

Go to www.1001DarkNights.com for more information.

HIDDEN INK by Carrie Ann Ryan
BLOOD ON THE BAYOU by Heather Graham
SEARCHING FOR MINE by Jennifer Probst
DANCE OF DESIRE by Christopher Rice
ROUGH RHYTHM by Tessa Bailey
DEVOTED by Lexi Blake
Z by Larissa Ione
FALLING UNDER YOU by Laurelin Paige
EASY FOR KEEPS by Kristen Proby
UNCHAINED by Elisabeth Naughton
HARD TO SERVE by Laura Kaye
DRAGON FEVER by Donna Grant
KAYDEN/SIMON by Alexandra Ivy/Laura Wright
STRUNG UP by Lorelei James
MIDNIGHT UNTAMED by Lara Adrian
TRICKED by Rebecca Zanetti
DIRTY WICKED by Shayla Black
THE ONLY ONE by Lauren Blakely
SWEET SURRENDER by Liliana Hart

About CD Reiss

CD Reiss is an Audie Award winner and *New York Times* bestseller. She still has to chop wood and carry water, which was buried in the fine print. Her lawyer is working it out with God but in the meantime, if you call and she doesn't pick up, she's at the well, hauling buckets.

Born in New York City, she moved to Hollywood, California to get her master's degree in screenwriting from USC. In case you want to know, that went nowhere, but it did give her a big enough ego to try her hand at books.

She's been nicknamed the "Shakespeare of Smut," which is flattering enough for her to put it in a bio, but embarrassing enough for her not to tell her husband, or he might think she's some sort of braggart who's too good to chop a cord of wood.

If you meet her in person, you should call her Christine.

You can find more information on her at https://cdreiss.com.

King of Code
By CD Reiss
Now Available

From *New York Times* Bestselling author, CD Reiss, comes an all new, sexy tale of secrets, intrigue, betrayal, and a love worth crossing a continent for.

Taylor Harden is a man on the edge.
The edge of fame. The edge of untold wealth.
The edge of utter humiliation.

He built an unhackable system, and in front of everyone, it's hacked.
His reputation goes from king to goat in a split second. Boom. Like that.

Some dude in Barrington, USA (AKA Nowhere) has locked down Taylor's code, and if he doesn't get it back, he's going to be wearing a monkey suit for the rest of his life.

Except, this guy? This hacker from Nowhere? He's not a guy.

Harper Watson's all woman. And she has a plan for Taylor, his code, and his body.

* * * *

King of Code is the first book in a new series of standalones.

* * * *

I leaned over the balcony rail to see her. Harper looked up from ground level, shielding her eyes from the sun. Her hair was in a loose ponytail at the back of her neck.

"What are you doing?" she called.

"I'm not leaving until you give me what you took, and the

mushrooms were making me crazy. They grow behind the walls. It's... unnerving."

"Unnerving?"

I gripped the railing. *Are you doing this or not?* "Come up here, Harper."

I'd decided. I was doing this.

I pointed toward the doors on the other side of the balcony that led to the room I'd slept in the night before. I did not say please, and I did not ask a question. One of us was in charge, and it wasn't her. Even if she had the keys to my life on the little ring in her head, this wasn't working if she was the one calling the shots.

I washed my hands in the mycelium-free bathroom by my room. No time for a shower.

The stairs creaked. A pressure grew behind my balls because I knew what was coming.

She stood at the end of the hall, hand draped on the bannister. Branches of hair had escaped her ponytail and dropped to either cheek. I pointed at a spot on the floor in front of me. She scratched a spot on her neck, which was unremarkable except for her hand. It looked as if it had been rinsed in light blue paint and scrubbed. The tinge was in the corners of the nails and the deep lines in her wrist.

"Come into my room and close the door," I said.

"You're all sweaty."

"You want to do this or not?"

If I had been trying to scare her, I'd failed. She practically skipped into the room.

"Close the door," I commanded again. She did it. "I want to set the rules right off."

"Okay."

"You won't tell me why you want this or why you went to all the trouble, but if you're trying to trap me into marriage or some shit—"

She laughed derisively. "Yeah. No."

My feelings were not hurt.

Nope.

Not one bit.

"Condoms." I put up a finger. "Every time."

"Yes."

I put up a second finger. "Don't come to me with emotional attachment. I'm not interested."

"Me neither."

My third finger made a W. "This has to be done in nine days. If it's not, I'm leaving, and I'll just deal with the consequences."

"It won't take longer than that. I told you. I'm a really good student."

"All right. Let's get this show on the road."

I dug my thumb into my other palm absently, thinking this might not be a bad way to spend a few days. QI4 would be back, Deepak would spin it into a learning experience; we'd work on manufacturing our own goddamn monitors and BIOS. I could just go back to the way things were. That alone was enough to give me serious wood.

"Take your clothes off, Harper."

On behalf of 1001 Dark Nights,

Liz Berry and M.J. Rose would like to thank ~

Steve Berry
Doug Scofield
Kim Guidroz
Jillian Stein
InkSlinger PR
Dan Slater
Asha Hossain
Chris Graham
Fedora Chen
Kasi Alexander
Jessica Johns
Dylan Stockton
Richard Blake
BookTrib After Dark
and Simon Lipskar

71463347R00071

Made in the USA
Lexington, KY
20 November 2017